I0699112

Dedicated to

Aaron and Luminita, two characters that continually surprise me and continue to weave an incredible tale of pain and love. I am simply in awe of what they've accomplished.

Jennifer Saviano my best friend and biggest supporter. These novellas simply would not exist without you. Thank you for continually pushing me to take risks and follow the story, no matter how dark the path.

Danny Nagel and **Kayla Bowers**, my test bunnies, I owe you so much. Without your incredible feedback, ideas, and support I'd be lost. Thank you so much!

Your mental health matters. Some may find this as a checklist of endorsements, but for those who have triggers, please read this list carefully.

Trigger Warnings include but are not limited to:

Strong violence & murder
Strong domestic violence
Sexual assault within a marriage
Non-consensual drug use
Strong sexual content
Depictions of war
Trauma response
Vivid and violent nightmares
Suicidal thoughts/ideation

This is a work of Fiction.
Although historic dates, circumstances, places, and people are used, they are done so in a fictitious manner and in no way reflect accurate history.
As far as we know.

Pronunciation/Translation Guide

This novella is set in Medieval Romania and uses historically accurate names, places, and Romanian words.

Pronunciation/Translation Guide

Beszterce (Bez-tear-say) A large palatial city of Wallachia, home of John Hunyadi, Regent of Hungary

Bălteni (Bluh-teen-e) City where Vlad II was killed

Dacians (Dah-key-ans) An ancient Agrarian society in Dacia (Romania)

Dogrugoz (Dog-rew-go-z) A city in Turkey where Vlad was imprisoned

Draga (Drah-gah) Romanian for "Beloved"

Dragaica (Drag-ache-ah) Romanian Lady of Flowers, a mythical fairy

Dragobete (Drag-oh-beat) Romanian festival of love and fertility

Kosovo Polje (Ko-so-vo Pole-yay) A valley in southern Serbia

Meu/Mea (may-ew/may-uh) Romanian for "my"

Mircea (Meer-cha) Vlad's eldest brother

Poiana Negrii (Poh-ah-nah Neg-ree) A small village between Beszterce and Suceava

Prelates - A bishop or other high dignitary of the clergy

Prostul moare de grija alutia (Pro-stool moor-a de gree-jah ah-loo-tee-ah)- The fool dies worrying about someone else

Sălbatic (sal-bah-tic) Romanian for "savage"

Şeytan (Shay-tahn) Turkish for "Devil"

Sibiu (Si-bee-oo) A city in Central Romania

Smederevo (Smed-eh-rev-oh) City in Serbia with a massive fortress

Stjpan Tomas (Step-ahn Toe-mahs) Bosnian ruler

Strigoi (stree-goy) a Romanian vampire

Suceava (Suhk-ee-vuh) A sprawling palace in Moldova

Szeged (Seh-ged) City in Hungary

Târgovişte (Tare-goo-vish-tay) A major city containing the palace of the Dracul family

Tigani boieresti (Tah-gah-nee boy-eh-rest-ee) Roma slaves of the Boyar (Noble) families

Turnu Roşu (Tour-new Row-shoo) A pass through the Southern Carpathian Mountains

Voivode (voy-vowd) A local ruler of a principality or province

Wallachia (Wa-lah-she-uh) A large Romanian province north of the Danube and South of the Carpathian Mountains
Timisoara (Tee-mee-sow-ah-rah) Romanian city along the Timis river

Draga &
The Savage:
Dracul

by Jenny Allen

Jenny Allen Books
York, PA 17408

1.   A Smaller World

Luminita
Suceava – October 1448

Since leaving Deva that fateful night over two hundred years ago, the world has gotten smaller. Villages became towns, towns turned into cities, castles and fortresses of stone now dot the landscape, and it has become harder to hide.

The legends of Dragaica have dwindled to mere stories, and the rising prominence of the Roman Catholic and Orthodox Churches has brought rumors of savage witch trials. Not only are people less inclined to believe in my readings and performances, but they have also become dangerous. Any display of my power, even in self-defense, is a risk, and I am no longer capable of sustaining myself as I have for hundreds of years.

The world is changing, and I must adapt. Avoiding humans is no longer the best way to control my fate. I must hide among them, stealing small bits of emotion unnoticed. I must plot and scheme, navigate the political waters, manipulate things to my advantage, and take an active part in shaping my world.

Unfortunately, this requires a man.

Unmarried women are capable of little more than the *tigani boieresti*— the Roma slaves belonging to the powerful boyar families, the royal lines who own the land. As with unmarried women, they are legally *human*, not property, but hold no rights.

I loathe the concept of even feigning the appearance of submission and adopting the demure etiquette required by the courts. I am an ancient goddess of blood and chaos among the weak, but survival is all that truly matters. I have sacrificed for it before…

My fingers trace along my neck, and the fragile imprint is barely detectable upon my skin. The fury and hatred were so palpable once…the curse I was forced to endure because of my actions on Dragobete so many years ago.

However, over time, the imprint of his emotions became a comfort, a reminder of his existence, and a warning to never again consider granting a man true power over me.

My thoughts often drift to my Savage, wondering if he still stalks the earth. In all these years, we have never again crossed paths, and I could not bring myself to look for him.

With a heavy sigh, I smooth the lines of my red dress. The corset and square neckline show enough cleavage to be enticing without being risqué. An oval ruby rests in the hollow of my throat, suspended on a gold chain. The stone is the wrong shape, but that is best. A reminder of what is lost forever will not help me advance my schemes.

I can play a part among these short-lived humans and pull the prideful strings of men. The politics may be more complex, but individual men are easy to manipulate.

Part of crafting the illusion required choosing a name more befitting of a delicate maidan. Luminita has been a whisper among the people, nearly synonymous with Dragaica, and the noble Dragomir name still intimidates some.

For this dance to succeed, I must be underestimated. While that is an inherent result of being a beautiful, seemingly young woman in these times, orchestrating events in the Suceava court in Moldova takes a delicate hand and an innocent façade, which cannot be called into question.

The persona of Katharina Siegel, the daughter of the Weaver's Guild noble south of Bucharest, is the definition of lilting femininity. She dances with lords, whispers sweet things, and takes advice from *older* women of repute. It disgusts me to no end, playing this part each night, but I have no choice in this patriarchal dictatorship.

In the past few months since arriving in Suceava, I've caught the eye of several nobles, three of whom have proposed marriage, but none of them carry enough clout to tempt me. Re-marrying is near impossible. I must choose my target carefully or risk falling victim to my own schemes.

Not a single one has possessed the strength I truly crave. My brief time in Deva left me desperate for the challenge…for a man to pose a true threat…for a worthy opponent. Of course, no human man is capable of that. It is likely an itch I will never again scratch.

I have not encountered another strigoi, and I have avoided the other Durand. The males of my kind are even more callous and ruthless toward women than humans. Therefore, I am forced to find contentment in the minds of simple human men.

New arrivals are expected at tonight's feast, according to the new Moldovan Voivode, Peter the Third. He began his rule after deposing Roman the Second, who was a mere twenty-two years of age. Peter is not much older and has a rather loose tongue when it pertains to court gossip.

According to the Voivode, a Wallachian noble who failed to take back his usurped throne is due to arrive tonight, seeking asylum in his court. The newcomer does not sound promising, but I have been surprised before…once at least.

After caressing my neck, savoring the final traces of the imprint, I straighten and pull on the mask of polite innocence I've carefully crafted. Whatever it takes to secure my future…to control my fate…to survive. No price is too high.

My fingertips drift between my breasts where a tear-shaped ruby once dangled. The ghost of it still clings to my skin. I've proven the price I'm willing to pay for my freedom…my heart and soul. Love is fleeting, but I have the potential for eternal life, even if it's as nothing more than a wicked creature pulling strings to achieve power. After all, power enables survival where love only puts it at risk.

2. Bogdan

Aaron
Kosovo Polje – October 1448

I strongly dislike retreat. Allowing *humans* to chase me away is a personal insult after seven thousand years as a vampire. I'm not the only one, but I am the oldest. Yet here I am, retreating from a sea of soldiers.

I grip the sword tighter as we race through the forest. The blood coating every inch of my body feels tacky, and my muscles burn. After three grueling days of fierce battle and losing far too many men, the Voivode of Wallachia and Regent of Hungary, John Hunyadi, called for the retreat.

I have never respected a human. Their lives are too brief to even garner my interest most times, but John is the closest a human has come to earning my regard. War is in his blood, and his strategic mind is sharper than most. Well, perhaps not in this *specific* instance.

This time, he underestimated the Ottoman forces and their allies. They overwhelmed us. No overwhelm is too generous a word. It was slaughter. Thousands upon thousands of our men died.

Now John and I are racing for Beszterce with only a handful of men.

Chaos and the clang of swords erupt to my right flank…John's direction. I swerve toward the conflict, sprinting like a blood-soaked devil between the evergreens. As I fly toward the fray, my left hand touches my armor and the small object hidden beneath the scales at the center of my chest. It's habit now, especially when facing danger. I've already suffered life's deepest wounds, and my heart still beats.

Jenny Allen

When I burst into the small clearing, John and three of his men are surrounded but still fighting. These are not soldiers of the Ottoman Empire, however. The color accenting their chainmail and tunics identify them as Serbian. Fantastic. Another one of John's enemies.

Without hesitation, I grip the pommel of my sword with both hands and slash up, catching the first soldier under the helmet. The brutal hit against the chainmail vibrates up my already weary arms, but the man's head flops to his shoulder with a sickening crack before he crashes to the ground.

Two men rush in my direction, side by side, and I don't hide my wicked smile as I relax into a fighting stance. When they're close enough, I parry the first blow, spinning to thrust my sword straight into the second man's throat, the blade scraping the jawbone before hitting his spine.

I don't hear the gargled sounds as he chokes, but the warmth from the blood splashing my skin when I yank the sword free makes my grin widen. The first soldier recovers his balance and lunges at me. I easily dodge the blow and hack downward with my blade with such power, the metal helmet dents deeply, cracking his skull. Blood pours down his face, and his body thuds to the ground.

A sharp sting at my thigh has me spinning to block another slicing cut. Our swords clang, and the man tries to push back. A waste of time. I slam my armored fist into his face, breaking the stalemate, and shove my blade up under his chin until the tip hits the inside of his helmet.

"Bogdan!" John shouts.

I use my boot to shove the Serb off my sword and move deeper into the melee, following John's voice. I sustain a few nicks while trudging through, but take out five more men. They aren't as well-trained as my recent opponents. The Serbs counted on numbers to overtake us.

I break through the line and see John being carted off. Apparently, numbers won after all.

At least a dozen men still swarm the area…all targeting me. An absolutely ruthless grin splits my blood-soaked face. The odds are *not* in their favor. I am Aaron, Bogdan the gift of god, Sălbatic the Savage. Blood is what I crave, and I will drink my fill today.

3.   Vlad Dracul

Luminita
Suceava – October 1448

I hover around the edge of the court, sifting through the sea of various emotions rippling through the room. Some are more common than others in this place. Pride, Lust, Envy, Gluttony, Sloth…most of the sins labeled by the Roman Catholic Church as deadly. They are far more common than the church leads people to believe.

Crowds have become easier to navigate these past few years. I've learned to gather a general feel of the place and then isolate the ones I desire. I study individual interactions, taking note of the malice lingering behind a warm smile, the disgust accompanying a young woman's laugh, even the fear that surrounds the Voivode Peter.

I don't blame the man. This court has changed hands violently several times since my arrival. There is always someone hungrier, someone greedier, waiting to slit the throat of the prince and take his position.

I don't notice when the newcomer from Wallachia arrives. The whispered rumors reach my ears first, spreading through the court like wildfire. A young man held captive with his younger brother in Dogrugoz. His father murdered in the marshes of Bălteni after failing to defend his crown. An older brother blinded and buried alive in Târgoviște.

It does not take long for fear to soak the crowd like a cold winter rain. Silence falls over the court until each heavy footstep echoes through the room. I find myself curious for the first time in ages. The masses part, allowing someone to approach the dais, and I slip past people until I have a proper view.

The man is young indeed, perhaps eighteen years of age, but no one could mistake him for innocent. There is a purposefulness to his stride, a hard set to his broad shoulders, and a firm grimace locked in place. What he lacks in height, he makes up for with strength beneath the somewhat dated finery. The equine nose somehow adds to his fierce appearance, but none of those things is what captures my attention.

Darkness and hunger cling to him like a second skin. It isn't ancient like…Sălbatic's had been back in Deva, but it has a similar feel. Younger. Less potent, but there, nonetheless.

I watch with interest while he approaches Peter and speaks quietly with him. The Voivode nods, and the stranger turns to face the court, standing straight with his proud shoulders pulled back.

"Subjects and nobles!" Peter exclaims, as if everyone's attention wasn't already firmly fixed on them. "I have granted asylum here at the court of Suceava in Moldova to the former Voivode of Târgoviște, Vlad Dracul the third. He is to be welcomed at my court." After his half-hearted decree, Peter waves a dismissive hand at his new guest.

Vlad directs his dark stare on the crowd, watching the people with a studious expression. Nearly every soul averts their eyes or suddenly finds something interesting to discuss, as if the man's gaze alone can inflict pain. Or perhaps, and more likely, they do not wish to invite an interaction with him.

When Vlad's gaze falls on me, I meet it fiercely. Some instincts are harder to break than others. Never show an enemy weakness. The lesson was drilled into me as a child. Of course, it is not a quality befitting a wilting flower…a proper lady…a demure subject. Sometimes the act is the most tedious part.

The man's intense eyes fix on me as he paces down the stairs, heading in my direction. The closer he comes, the more delectable the darkness, and a smile stretches my lips, which is far from the shy one I've practiced.

"You meet a man's gaze as if you are his equal?" The question sounds gruff in his gravelly tone, but curiosity emerges from the depths of his emotional well.

I lower my eyes and bow my head, as all proper ladies should, but then peer up at him through my lashes. "No, sir. Of course, I am not your equal." I am no one's equal in this room…this city. I far surpass them all.

Draga & the Savage: Dracul

Thick black lashes frame his bluish-grey eyes. They are rather striking. Although without the blue they'd resemble… I stamp out the thought before it fully forms.

"Vlad Dracul the Third of Wallachia," he holds out his hand, palm up. "And you are?"

"Katharina Siegel, sir." When I slip my hand into his, lust surges past the dark hunger lurking in him. It is not unexpected. Physical contact at court, at least in public, is not all that common between strangers.

The young man keeps his eyes on me as he bends to place a kiss on the back of my hand. He studies me as if trying to understand a new species. A rather apt metaphor now that I think of it.

"I am very pleased to make your acquaintance, Miss Katharina." Vlad stands up straight, and even though he is shorter than some men, he's still slightly taller than me.

When I don't correct his assumption of me being unwed, a smile unfurls across his lips. For some reason, it doesn't suit him.

I glance around us to witness everyone either openly staring or actively trying to avoid notice. It makes me feel rather bold. "Hmm…you'd think by such a reaction, a strigoi had landed in our midst." I keep my eyes on the crowd to feign innocence, but the potent spike of fear and nervousness provides my answer.

I turn back to Vlad with a brilliant smile. "It's about time someone made this court interesting."

"And you have not accomplished that already?"

I pull on another smile and shrug softly. The motion makes the ruby at my throat glint, capturing his gaze, but it quickly returns to my face.

"I prefer…smaller crowds…less noise."

Vlad holds his arm out to me in invitation. "I do not care much for the attention of sycophants and the morally destitute. They bring out a darkness in me. Shall we walk?"

"With such talk of darkness, how could a lady resist?" I bat my eyes playfully, and a sound almost like a laugh escapes him.

"I mean you no harm, Katharina."

I loop my arm through his with a curious grin. "But you do wish someone harm?"

He considers me for a moment and, once again, appears far older than his years. "Would it scare you if my answer is yes?" he asks quietly.

I hold his burning gaze and slowly shake my head.

Desire and excitement tingle over his skin. It's not the sensation I crave most…not the blend that truly makes my heart race, but it is something I can use to my benefit. Men are tools after all, nothing more. Longing and foolish notions of love are for children.

We retire to a quiet corner and watch the other courtiers revel.

"I am curious," he says in his low, gruff voice. "What do you know of the strigoi?"

I stand beside him, my eyes still fixed on the room before us. "I met one once…a long time ago." Despite my best efforts, melancholy leaks into my voice, but Vlad doesn't seem to notice.

"And yet you live?" The disbelief is rather clear.

"Of course. He never bit me, only those that harmed me…or when he hungered, but never me."

His amusement transforms into intrigue. "You tell the truth?"

I lean a little closer to whisper, but not so near that I might cause a scandal. "Can you keep a secret?"

The man's intense eyes widen in surprise before a smile tugs at his lips. He nods.

"I saved the strigoi's life and he owed me a debt."

A frown wrinkles the young man's stern brow. "Why would you save such a creature?"

Once again, I meet his inquisitive stare with a bold confidence most find unladylike. "Unique creatures should not be punished for what they are. There is beauty even in darkness."

Vlad's stare heats with a ravenous glint, providing further proof. There is violence within him he wishes to embrace, but thus far, imprisonment and political maneuverings have curtailed his urges. The hunger lingers there, too. Vlad Dracul is a strigoi, and I have captured his attention. Most women would be terrified, but I am no mere woman.

4. Value of a Moment

Aaron
Smederevo – December 1448

Smederevo Fortress is a striking reminder of the capabilities of *human* ingenuity. I don't appreciate the short-lived things often, but the sprawling structure of smooth stone walls, turrets, and towers is rather monumental.

Archers watch me warily from the four sets of double-arched windows at the Danube entrance to the fortress, arrows nocked and waiting. I do not dismount my horse or make any sudden moves to provoke them. I am not immune to arrows, and today I am not a warrior. I am an emissary.

Durad Brankovic, the Despot of Serbia, has kept my Voivode, John Hunyadi, prisoner in the bowels of this place for nearly two months. As his closest confidant, second in command, and most highly decorated soldier, I have been tasked with delivering his ransom and escorting John home to Beszterce.

Fully armored guards march across the bridge, their chainmail clinking while their boots stomp heavily on the wood. I remain perfectly still on my warhorse, Kali, while the men retrieve the sacks of gold florins from John's horse.

The few nervous glances they cast my way indicate my reputation on the battlefield precedes me. I don't fight my feral grin. The men seem to move faster and quickly hustle across the bridge to the relative safety of their fortress.

Jenny Allen

Time passes slowly, and I flex my hand around the saddle's pommel while keeping my eyes on the gate. A small crowd of peasants peer out curiously, but no other movement.

Brankovic does not have a reputation for being a trusting soul. He is most likely having his men count each florin before releasing Hunyadi.

My hand drifts to the center of my armor and the object hidden beneath its scales. The habit is not just reserved for battle. It's rather common when my mind is free to roam and memories hover in the edges of my consciousness.

Some days, it feels like another life. After two hundred years, perhaps it qualifies as exactly that. Other days, the memories unfold behind my eyes as if they occurred mere days ago. Tears flooding hypnotic sea-blue eyes still haunt my dreams on a near-nightly basis, regardless.

The crowd around the gate begins to move, drawing my attention back to the present and away from conflicting memories. John Hunyadi emerges from the gate, flanked by soldiers.

The man's receding hair is almost shaggy, a short beard blends into his thick moustache, and dark circles encompass his red-rimmed eyes. His two-month captivity was probably not a pleasant one, judging by his disheveled appearance. Even amid war, John has never appeared weak as he does now, approaching with his shoulders slumped in defeat. Before Deva, I might have held that against him.

I notice the guards halt at the end of the bridge. Apparently, they are not eager to get close now that I have what I want. Not *all* humans are stupid, it seems.

"Bogdan." John nods a greeting, exhales a deep breath, and slowly mounts his horse with a grimace. "You could have brought a wagon," he grumbles.

"And you could have avoided capture."

The man's eyes narrow at me with an icy glare.

I shrug and guide my horse away from Smederevo. The man does not keep me around for placating words of comfort. "Hauling you away in a wagon would have only made you appear weaker, John."

A long sigh escapes as he guides his horse to trot beside mine. "You speak true, as always, my friend. This ordeal has been humiliating enough."

"Are you injured?" I ask.

John shakes his head. "Nothing I haven't survived before. Brankovic didn't wish to harm me too much. He intended to hand me over to the

Ottoman Empire, and they would have taken offense to receiving *damaged goods*."

"Why didn't he?"

"Many of the Hungarian barons and prelates assembled at Szeged and persuaded him to make peace with me. It would be far more lucrative." The man's top lip twists into a snarl. "Bloody jackals, the lot of them."

"I'm assuming this cost you more than 100,000 florins?"

John rubs a hand over his face. "I had to relinquish all the domains we've seized from him. This will severely weaken my position as Regent and Voivode."

"You are a man of war, John. You were not born to sit upon a throne and entertain the insignificant squabbles of commoners. You live for the blood, the challenge, just as I do."

A huff escapes the man. "You're still young, Bogdan. I'm forty-two years old. I may not have many more battles in me."

The hilarity of his unknown error is not lost on me. I may have survived over seven thousand years, but I still look younger than John. The minuscule streaks of grey in my long dark hair are the only indication I'm older than thirty.

"Sad words by a tired man. The battle frenzy is not finished with you, my friend." *Friend.* The word feels odd on my tongue. For thousands of years, I never bothered to have an actual conversation with a human, much less befriend one. What is the point? Their lives are a mere blink in my existence.

However, my experience in Deva taught me the value of a moment. Less than three days changed my entire existence, forever altering my course. After two hundred years, their importance has not dwindled.

I still do not make a habit of entertaining humans. Most of them still disgust me if I consider them at all, but John Hunyadi shares my bloodthirsty spirit. Being his second in command has allowed me to embrace my violence.

The men find my barbaric tactics inspiring, and the enemy fears any battleground I set foot upon. I drink my fill while fighting the Turks. It is the ideal situation for a vampire such as myself.

"So, what is the plan?" I ask, knowing he has one. Despite his claims of being tired, the man's mind is perpetually stuck on battle.

We ride in silence for a time while John wears a contemplative expression.

"We return home, rest, regroup, secure what power I have within the court…"

A grin stretches my lips. "And then?"

John's red-rimmed eyes slide to me with calculated fury. "We march on the traitorous bastard John Jiskra, for breaking the armistice. The truce-breaking Czech deserves a lesson."

I lean over to clap a hand on John's shoulder with a hearty laugh. "There's my bloodthirsty friend."

5.   Husband

Luminita
Suceava – September 1449

I watch Vlad pace around our room, pulling on clothes with a troubled expression. His irritation about being stranded at the Suceava court has only grown in the past months. Not even sex seems to calm him these days.

I sprawl out on my naked stomach and rest my chin in my palm. "What troubles you today, Vlad?" I ask, feigning interest. I already know the answer. The frustration itching beneath his skin is familiar and unmistakable.

Vlad pauses while fastening his pants. Dark hair curls over his broad chest as it heaves. He is an attractive specimen and not unskilled at fornicating, but it is all a calculated dance without the distraction of feelings. At least, on my part. Vlad, however, feels a great deal.

Hunger lights his blue-grey eyes despite our recent romp beneath the sheets. "Katharina." A warning infuses his gruff voice, one that irritates me.

"If you intend to lecture me again on how a woman has no business in politics, save your breath. You know my counsel is better than the simple-minded men of this court."

Vlad forgoes his shirt and paces back to the bed. He bends low to press a lingering kiss against my lips. "You do have a fascinating mind, my wife." The low rumble of his voice is pleasant but doesn't heat my blood. I use the clear memory of someone else to summon the blush to my cheeks and complete the façade of an enamored wife.

"If you wish to reclaim your throne…" I begin.

Vlad sits back on his heels, watching me fiercely.

"You must gather support in Wallachia."

His lips press into a thin line. "There is no insight in that statement, Katharina." He moves to stand, but I grab his muscled arm.

"I'm not finished."

The glare is sharp and wicked this time, and I resist the urge to draw on his essence. I could put this man on his knees in the blink of an eye. He has no idea of the power I possess…the dangerous creature he lies vulnerable beside each night.

"Please," I say, forcing a demure tone past my lips.

After releasing a weary sigh that further tempts me to bring the half-blood strigoi to heel, he sits upon the mattress and gestures for me to continue.

I force the annoyance from my voice. "Write to the Voivode of Wallachia and seek permission to speak with him at his court in Beszterce. If you can gain his support, perhaps he will back your claim."

Rage fills the air in a stifling flood. Vlad surges to his feet with a sneer twisting his unusually handsome face. "John Hunyadi ordered the execution of my father and eldest brother. He turned the boyar families against us. *Then* he gave *my* throne to that bastard Vladislav. I will *not* beg for his help!"

I rise to sit on the bed, unashamed of my naked form. Lust perfumes his signature, dimming his anger enough to listen. "Then you are a fool," I state plainly.

Fury overtakes everything, and he raises his hand to strike me. I catch his arm with a hateful glare of my own.

"I may value your dark cravings and violence, husband, but strike me, and it will be the last thing you ever do."

Although my strength shocks him, it is not outside the realm of possibility, like my Durand powers to sense and feed on emotion. Besides, Vlad would never admit to being bested by a woman, so the threat of persecution is minimal in this case.

After locking eyes intently, he withdraws a step.

"Now may I continue?" I ask, raising one eyebrow.

Begrudgingly, Vlad nods, his dark hair spilling over his sculpted shoulders.

"Thank you. Your attempt to take back the throne…the one that led you here…to me, was valiant. From what I know—"

"What do you know, wife? How do you know any of this? I have not spoken about my failed campaign." Suspicion clouds his eyes. Sometimes his paranoia is exhausting.

"I listen at court while others dismiss me as a mere woman. I do *not* occupy their beds, Vlad. I am sworn to you and you alone."

The suspicion lessens but never disappears. He is a watchful and possessive man who never lets me stray far.

"John Hunyadi admires strength in battle above all else."

"I *lost* the last battle, Katharina. I lost the crown."

"*Because* you did not have the support of the Voivode and boyar families, *not* because of *your* strength and ferocity. Go to court, build a rapport with the man, earn his trust. Once you have the throne, you can exact whatever revenge you desire."

He studies me with the calculating stare I've grown to admire. Vlad may be quick to violence, but he is capable of being quite devious. "I will write and test the waters. A response may take some time. Hunyadi prefers to lead his armies, and the last I heard, he was marching on—"

"John Jiskra," I interrupt.

Vlad's scowl morphs into a slight smile beneath his thick moustache. "You are a singular woman, Katharina…unlike any I've met."

"I suppose that makes you a lucky man," I coo with a seductive grin.

Vlad slips back onto the bed beside me, his fingertips tracing down the graceful curve of my spine. "I suppose we shall see." His tender touch trails back up, sinking into my hair. It's pleasant, but not overly so.

Then, Vlad's fingers curl tight in my hair and force my head back to meet his stony gaze. "I admire your fire, wife. But do not threaten my life again. Men have died for less."

Keeping the righteous hatred out of my eyes is a distinct challenge. "Yes, husband." The words sicken me. Pretending to be subservient, knowing I can snatch control at any time, and choosing not to, is almost worse than giving over dominion of my life.

His kiss is bruising and thorough but lacks the passion that once swept me up…the energy that almost persuaded me to let go completely. Vlad enjoys it, but I merely endure it. This is the price of pulling strings as a woman…the ultimate role I am reduced to.

No matter how sound my logic, how keen my strategy, I am nothing more than a means to physical pleasure…a repository for his useless hopes for an heir. The Durand are not a fertile species, and from what I've learned, neither are the strigoi.

Eventually, I will have to plan an escape. As is the case with most things, infertility is blamed on the woman with violent repercussions.

6.   The Great Barbarian

Aaron
Beszterce Court – December 1449

Excitement tingles over my skin while I stalk toward John's quarters in Beszterce. A summons to see him typically involves plotting another bloody campaign, and I'm eager to wash away the taste of failure.

The raids and attacks on John Jiskra's lands reduced his forces, but ultimately, we had no choice but to retreat...*again*. The Czech mercenaries were too great a challenge for our soldiers, and one great Barbarian cannot defeat an entire army on his own.

When I reach John's door, I draw in a deep breath to ease the anxious tension in my chest. Staying here at the court is merely biding my time until the next battle. I hate the complacency of this place.

While smoothing the lines of my simple blue linen shirt, a frown wrinkles my brow. I've never cared for the finery of the court either. They are little more than costumes meant to fluff the fragile egos of insignificant men. However, John prefers I dress the part. He will simply be disappointed today.

My sharp knock is immediately met with a shout to enter. He seems rather impatient. That bodes well for me.

"Bogdan, good." John sighs in relief and continues to pace with a letter clutched in his hand. He appears worried. Perhaps this will not be a good day for me after all.

"How may I be of service, General?"

John stops and peers at me as if I've said something odd. "We are not on the battlefield, Bogdan. Within these walls, I am Voivode."

I straighten and clear my throat. Humans have such idiotic rules. "My apologies, Voivode." I force the words. I respect John's battle acumen, not his pompous title.

The man waves a hand and cracks a smile. "In my quarters, it's simply John or friend."

A slight smile tugs at my lips, and I nod. "Of course, my friend. How may I be of assistance?"

With an aggravated groan, John holds up the letter in his clenched fist. "I don't trust the upstart." He resumes pacing, his face turning red.

I lean against the door, arms crossed over my chest. "I'm afraid you'll need to be more specific, John."

"Vlad Dracul the third. He's requesting an audience here at my court."

I've heard rumblings of the man, none of them good. "Explain your hesitation to accept."

"I had his father killed for one," the man blurts in frustration.

"Valid. And?"

"His elder brother, Mircea. I made an example of him. Blinded him with iron stakes and buried him alive in Târgoviște."

My eyebrows rise. "Quite creative. I approve."

John unsuccessfully hides a smirk. "I suppose that is your style."

"The stakes, perhaps," I admit. "I'm not fond of burying my prey, though."

The man shrugs and starts moving again.

"So, you worry this Vlad character is seeking revenge?"

"Wouldn't you be worried?"

"No," I reply simply.

The man stops, turns on his heel, and stares at me as if I've spontaneously grown a second head.

"*You* are the Voivode of Wallachia, Regent of Hungary. You have troops, guards, hell…you have me." A savage grin splits my mouth. "Vlad has been hiding at the Suceava court. He has no men, no resources."

"I don't know that for certain, Bogdan." With a thoughtful frown, John rubs at his thick moustache. "He's recently married, and I have no information on his wife or her family. The treaties with Stjpan Tomas and Bogdan the second—" He throws a suspicious glare at me. "Are you certain you aren't related to him, by the way?"

A chuckle escapes, and I hold out my hands. "I am *quite* certain, John. I have *no* relatives in Romania."

Draga & the Savage: Dracul

The man's heavy brow scrunches. "Yet you hail from here. Unnatural."

I bite back a grin and merely shrug. He has no idea how correct he is.

"That's beside the point." His hand waves through the air again. "The treaties have strengthened my position somewhat, but Vladislav, the man who currently wears the Dracul crown, is becoming a problem. I'd take the position for myself, but it would stretch me too thin. The boyar families want someone strong."

"So, you are considering backing the man whose life you destroyed?" I ask in amusement. Humans have the most ridiculous logic at times.

"Perhaps. The boyars didn't back him before because he was too young, and they questioned his loyalty after I placed Vladislav in power. Vlad tried to take the crown by force a few years ago. Had he garnered proper support, he would have succeeded."

"And what are your concerns beyond his possible vendetta against you?"

One brow raises as he tilts his head. "I'm sure you know the story."

After dragging in a slow breath, I force a smile. "Explain it as if I never pay attention at court."

A hearty laugh fills the room. "Bogdan, what am I to do with you?" After shaking his head, he continues. "The man spent eight years as a prisoner of the Ottoman Empire. Murad the Second kept Vlad and his younger brother, Radu, in Gallipoli and then Dogrugoz. Vlad was only ten when his father gave him to Murad. I still recall the man's words. *Please understand that I have allowed my children to be butchered for the sake of the Christian peace.* I do not regret having killed the man."

"Hmm. I suppose that explains things," I say while pushing away from the door. "The few bits I've heard about Vlad Dracul the third—when I *actually* pay attention—claim he's not fond of the church and leans toward…unusual proclivities. Pain, torment, that sort of thing. All well and good on the battlefield, but not so much in your home." At least by human expectations.

Although…I do not toy with my food anymore. Once upon a time, I might have drawn out their torment, but now I'm content to take what I need. Occasionally, I'll watch the life leak from their eyes, but it has always been a fascination with death more than a sadistic desire.

As for the penchant for sexual sadism, I have no real interest. There are very few humans I can tolerate being around for long, and none of them appeal to me sexually. They are mere food with an expiration date.

Only one person has ever enticed the lustful beast out of me, and she was *no mere woman*. Unfortunately, the longing feels just as acute as it did two hundred years ago. I don't even know if she still lives…my goddess of blood and chaos.

"I've heard the same," John says on a sigh. "Too bad for his new bride."

After taking a moment to shove away my melancholy thoughts, I ponder the dilemma. Human posturing and power plays are most likely the best course of action. "Invite him to court in a year's time. Allow him to consider his strategy and your willingness to hear him out. Then you can form an opinion."

John rubs his chin and nods. "Makes sense. Give him time to rethink any impetuous plans. I don't think one meeting will suffice, however."

"Then test the man's dedication to his cause. Keep inviting him to court, but do not grant him asylum here until you're certain of his loyalty. Become his political mentor. The boy is still young and moldable."

A grin cracks his face. "Why won't you accept land and a title from me? You are too smart to be a simple soldier."

I shrug. "Because I do not desire those things, my friend. I long for the kill…the blood and chaos of war, not *domestic bliss* and political grandstanding, no offense."

John bellows another laugh and claps a hand on my shoulder. "Bogdan, my dear friend! The way you harbor hatred for *domestic bliss* makes me think a *woman* broke the Great Barbarian Bogdan!"

I force a smile. The joke hits far too close to the mark. I rub at the small object hidden in the pocket sewn into my sleeve's cuff.

"It would take far more than a simple woman to break me." Which is true. Luminita was so much more than that.

"Well, my friend! That I do believe. We must find you a wife, perhaps then you'll accept my offer!"

I shake my head and try not to appear disgusted by the notion. "I have no need for a wife. Blood and Chaos are all that appeal to me."

7.   Sălbatic

Luminita
Beszterce court – March 1451

The moment we arrive at Beszterce, I am acutely…painfully aware of his presence, and my heart thunders in my chest. His signature…his ancient hunger clings to *everything*, and I'm breathless.

I follow Vlad on horseback toward the stables, but my mind is flooded with memories as vivid as the day they occurred…all of them, including the devastating ones. My hand drifts to my throat, but his anger no longer clings to my skin, and its absence feels even more torturous now.

"Katharina," Vlad barks when I sit stunned on my horse within the stable. "Are you unwell?" His sharp eyes narrow on me.

I flash a reassuring smile and push everything aside. "No," I reply softly while sliding out of the saddle into his rather impatient arms. "I'm merely tired from the ride."

With an almost gentle hand, he brushes a stray curl of my dark hair away from my face. "I am sorry we could not procure a cart. Five days' travel by horse is a lot for a woman."

My annoyance is more difficult to hide when surrounded by so many reminders of who I once was. "I'm fine," I reply in only a slightly clipped tone.

His gaze lingers on me a little too long before he addresses the servants, barking orders about our belongings and how to care for our horses…as if these people don't attend to these things daily.

I have no great love for humans. They are desperate, ravenous things with short, brutal lives, but Vlad's sense of entitlement and waste of energy aggravate me.

While he continues to dole out instructions, I smooth the layers of my sea-blue dress and lace-trimmed corset. I changed into the lavish thing this morning before we started the final leg of our journey. It was a luxurious gift from the Moldovan Voivode presented to me at my wedding. Vlad was not too thrilled by the gesture. Perhaps that's why this dress is my favorite.

I stare out at the buildings and their windows, wondering if he's watching, and if he is…will he try to harm me again? Two hundred years allows a lot of time for pain and heartache to harden into hate. Or perhaps he will live up to his declaration that day by the river when I said his claim of not caring was a lie. *Then I will hate you until it's true.* Maybe he will not care about my presence here. I am not sure which would feel worse, his hate or his indifference.

My gaze tracks over all the trailing imprints visible to me. It's thousands, if not more. Aaron spending so much time among humans seems…out of character with the man I knew. But then, it is an oddity for me as well. Perhaps he's found it just as necessary. Of course, that does not mean he'll maintain a civil façade if confronted by me.

"Are you sure you're well?" Vlad moves to stand in front of me and touches my cheek with genuine concern. Despite all his rough edges and darkness, the man does love me.

"Quite," I lie with a soft smile.

Vlad's gaze trails down my neck to the low-cut neckline of my corset, which displays more cleavage than my usual dresses. His fingers coast across the swell of my breasts, leaving a feral desire in their wake. "This dress might be a little *too* appealing."

The act succeeds in clearing my head. My stare hardens, but he's not looking at my eyes. "Does it matter what is on display if you are the only one permitted to touch it?"

Slowly, his blue-grey eyes lift back to mine. "Do not forget it, my love."

"As if I could," I snap impatiently. "When would you even allow me out of your sight?"

His strong jaw tenses until a muscle ticks in his cheek. "Do not test me, wife."

I pull on yet another sweet smile. I've pushed a little too far. The discomfort of this place has weakened my mask. "I shall be the very picture of demure femininity, my husband. Besides, we are attempting to display strength, and this is the finest dress I own." I press a kiss against his cheek and loop my arm through his.

A smile eases the tension in his face, and the violence in him recedes. However, as with his dark hunger and possessiveness, the violence is never gone. None of this bodes well with Aaron's presence here.

Part of me wants to run, but the goddess in me refuses to cower to any man, even Aaron. If he still holds malice in his heart, he can face mine as well.

We stroll across the grounds in the late afternoon sun, letting it warm the chill from our skin. Vlad says nothing more. He's typically a man of few words, much to my relief.

The guards stop us at the massive structure's entrance, and Vlad quickly relays our information. Once a servant arrives to escort us, the soldiers let us pass. Naturally, Vlad's anger rises when their gaze lingers on me longer than he'd like, but I ignore it all.

I move without truly absorbing details. Aaron *saturates* this place, suffocating me with his presence until my lungs feel like they may burst.

I pass mighty halls, grand oil paintings, elaborate candelabras…all the décor to stun the senses and display wealth, but I take no notice. Instead, I visually track the various paths Aaron has travelled through these halls.

A host of voices fill the air, becoming louder with each step, and I force myself to swallow down the apprehension flooding my system.

"Katharina." Vlad's voice shakes me from the odd trance, and I smile over at him. "You're trembling, my love."

I widen the smile and pat his arm. "Nerves, nothing more." It isn't a lie this time.

"*You* have nothing to be nervous about, my wife. You are a vision."

As if my only purpose is to be something pleasant to look at…an interesting bauble, but if that gaze lingers too long…

My smile is tight this time. "Nervous for you, husband. I only wish to see you succeed."

Vlad presses a chaste kiss to my lips before facing the court and leading me forward.

My gaze drifts through the gathered crowd, taking in the mixture of fear and curiosity, combined with spikes of lust. It does not take long for my senses to lead my eyes toward the dais.

A cluster of men is gathered in a heated discussion. One stands taller than the rest, dressed in a simple linen shirt of royal blue. My heart rages against my ribs with each step closer, and I'm unable to avert my eyes from the long dark hair streaked with faint traces of grey, the deep dimples bracketing his smile, or the strong lines of his powerful body. It's as if not a single day has passed since Dragobete.

With considerable effort, I shove every riotous emotion in the deep, dark pit in my mind and pull on the demure persona befitting Vlad Dracul's wife.

The men are still speaking as we ascend the stairs, and someone catches the attention of a short, but broad-shouldered man with a receding hairline. The well-dressed man's face cracks with a wide smile as he peers back at us.

"Vlad Dracul the Third! Welcome to my court!" He throws his arms wide and embraces my husband before turning his attention to me. "And this must be your new bride. How exquisite."

I extend my hand with a shy blush, and he places a kiss of greeting on the back of my hand.

"Allow me to introduce my top general, my second in command." The man, who must be John Hunyadi, motions to the cluster of men. "Bogdan! Come meet Vlad Dracul and his lovely wife…" He trails off and peers over at me, allowing me to supply my name.

"Katharina," I say as Aaron steps around the last man.

His light grey eyes immediately snap to mine and widen with shock. It's the only emotion pouring out of him, and that familiar energy hums seductively between us.

"Come on, man. You're a barbaric beast on the battlefield, but I know you have manners!" Hunyadi slaps Aaron hard on the back.

Aaron blinks, but says nothing, as if he's frozen.

Irritation and jealousy prick my senses from my husband's direction. The longer I allow this to play out, the more suspicious Vlad will become.

I drag on a pleasant smile. "Barbaric. Sounds rather savage. Perhaps *Sălbatic* is a more fitting name than Bogdan."

A smile tugs at the corner of Aaron's mouth, but the sudden flood of intense heat and desire in his eyes steals the breath from me. Hunyadi's boisterous laugh barely registers.

"What a delightful creature, Vlad. She's quite funny!" The Voivode claps my husband's shoulder. "Come. We should talk in private. Bogdan can look after your wife."

I swallow hard and force my gaze away from Aaron as Vlad's grip on my arm tightens. "I'd rather keep her with me," Vlad replies in a low, threatening tone.

Draga & the Savage: Dracul

John Hunyadi is not phased. He bellows another deep laugh. "Business is no place for a woman. Besides, Bogdan has no interest in the fairer sex, do you?"

Aaron straightens, drawing my attention once more. "No, sir." Then his gaze finds mine again with the weight of a physical touch. "I serve only the Goddess of Blood and Chaos." When his stare shifts to Vlad, the unmistakable flood of hatred and envy twists my stomach. "On the battlefield only, of course."

"See? Your wife is perfectly safe! No one in my court will harm a hair upon her head."

The dark pit in my mind roils and bubbles, threatening to spill over with a chaotic amalgamation of emotions too overwhelming to remain contained. Still, I manage to keep my polite smile in place as I turn to Vlad.

"I will be fine, husband."

The flicker of pain from Aaron at that title falling from my lips only worsens when I press a kiss to Vlad's cheek, and it almost weakens my resolve.

Vlad turns and whispers against my ear. "You are already aware of how I intend to deal with betrayers. Do *not* count yourself among them, my love."

The tight smile is all I can muster as I pull away. If we were not in the middle of court, I just might have lost control and drained him dry.

His scathing stare stays on me, however, expecting a response to his threat.

"Of course not," I respond before slipping my arm away from his.

Vlad holds my gaze for as long as he can while following Hunyadi.

Then I am alone in a sea of strangers with Aaron, Sălbatic, Ares incarnate, my Dionysus, who stares at me like a starving man.

8.   Lady Dracul

Aaron

"Lady Dracul." I force the proper words past my lips, even though they sicken me, and offer my arm.

Luminita stares at it for a moment, her chest rising and falling with heavy breaths. Then her face tilts up to mine with an icy glare that cuts right to my core.

"I do not think that is wise, Sir Bogdan."

That name on her lips makes my throat tighten. To her, I have always been Sălbatic. "I mean you no harm. I meant what I said about who I worship."

Begrudgingly, she slips her arm around mine, and the simple touch makes the cold, dead lump of flesh in my chest riot.

"You should be careful saying such things. It is not very Christian."

"No," I say as I lead her down the dais. "I suppose it is not." Memories of our Dionysian ritual dance through my head. Visions of her wrapped in sheer crimson, glimmering in the torchlight, chanting like some mythical creature.

"You've been here some time," she says as if stating a known fact. "Your signature…your impression drenches every inch of this place." The haunted tone of her voice implies it troubles her. I could ask, but I'm not sure I'd like the answer.

"For quite a while, yes. It is my home when not at war." I guide her toward the large windows overlooking the budding garden and away from the crowds. I remember how draining they can be on her. "I looked for you." The words leave my mouth despite every instinct not to say them.

"To exact your revenge, no doubt." She pulls her arm away and faces the window.

"No," I respond in a softer voice.

A huff escapes, and her hand drifts up to her throat almost absently. "Then I suppose you are a horrible tracker."

A smile cracks my mouth despite the sharp tone. Her fire is what attracted me to her in the first place, and I have desperately missed it.

"Did you ever look for me?" As soon as the question passes my lips, the air freezes in my lungs. She slowly turns to face me again. The rich hue of her dress only enhances the hypnotic sea-blue of her deep eyes, which narrow at me.

"No. If I had, I would not have failed."

The magnetic energy between us pulls me closer, but I somehow manage to maintain a civil distance. "Why not?" I whisper.

Her breath hitches, and the rather generous swell of her breasts tempts me as they rise with a deep breath. She is the most beautiful creature I've laid eyes on, and I am just as lost to her now as I was two hundred years ago.

Luminita grips my chin and forces me to meet her eyes. "Stop," she snaps.

"What would you like me to stop, Luminita?" The deep seductive tone of my voice surprises me, and I am not the only one.

The way her eyes widen, the dark of her eyes spreading to nearly eclipse the blue, her lips parting with a shallow breath, they all betray her attraction, and gods… It takes every ounce of strength not to kiss her.

She regains her composure faster than I do. Those sea-blue eyes turn to wicked points, and she takes a step back. "Katharina," she corrects me. "And I did not look for you because…." She turns away again, and it's like the sun sinking beneath the horizon, denying me its warmth. "Because you made things perfectly clear that morning. I submit to no one."

The last statement sounds hollow now. It's not the fierce declaration of a goddess. "Are you certain?"

Luminita glares over her shoulder with open contempt, but I continue regardless.

"Your *husband* would disagree, I'm sure." I don't hide my hatred for the word, or the pain it causes me. My offers weren't enough for her, but this brute's are? The familiar soul-rending heartache of that morning returns to me in full force. I was not enough.

She turns with her hand ready to strike, but I quickly grab her wrist and flash a bright smile to the crowd, despite my inner torment. "We are in the middle of court," I whisper beneath my breath. "If you strike me in public, no matter how justified, it will cause more trouble for you than me."

Luminita rips her arm from my grip but doesn't try again. "You know nothing of my marriage, *Sir Bogdan*." The woman's scathing tone stings more than a sword's slice.

"Perhaps not," I concede. "But I know of Vlad and his…tendencies."

She studies me as if trying to decipher my meaning. "You know?"

Confusion wrinkles my brow, and I lean slightly closer to whisper. "What do I know?"

Luminita blinks and peers around the room before whispering her answer. "He is a strigoi. Half, at least."

A derisive laugh rumbles from my throat, and I shake my head. "That makes sense on many levels. You do seem to have a penchant for collecting dark things."

Although she glares at me, it lacks true fury.

"Has he hurt you?" I ask, once again, unable to stop myself.

A faint blush graces her neck, but she straightens. "No," she lies. "Of course, not. I do not need your concern."

I lean back against the wall, arms crossing my chest to keep from touching her…from ripping her away from this place, away from *him*. "You have it regardless, Katharina."

She steps closer and stares up at me with such righteous fury it stirs everything in me at once. "Where was that concern when you were intent on forcing a confession from me?"

I swallow hard on the shame I've carried over that moment. I knew she feared losing control, and I was so blinded by my heartache that I nearly forced it from her. My head hangs low, and I try to find the words.

"I have never wanted anything in my long life as I wanted that night with you. Or since, for that matter. When that was taken from me…"

Luminita retreats a step, her gaze falling to the floor. "It is in the past," she says brusquely before facing the window again.

"Is it?" It certainly doesn't feel like it is. The pull, the magnetic energy that draws us together…it's just as strong as it was that night.

Her spine stiffens, but she says nothing.

I turn to stare out the window beside her, my arm grazing hers. The minuscule touch is bittersweet torment. "It isn't for me."

Although I hear the hard swallow, feel the tremble beneath her skin, her words cut like a knife. "Then you are a fool, as you have always been."

Despite *everything*…my hand caresses hers between us, out of sight from prying eyes. "Only for you."

The tear that streaks down her cheek sets my very soul on fire…the one I thought was dead forever.

"Don't," she says in an almost inaudible whisper. "Vlad is a possessive man. If anyone…" After pulling her hand from mine, she takes a step away.

Anger churns in my gut until my insides are twisted. "I am not afraid of Vlad Dracul."

Her eyes slowly lift to mine with a heart-stopping weight. "You are playing with human games now, and there is power in numbers. What you want does not matter. I belong to him."

"You cannot belong to a dead man." The declaration leaves my throat in a fierce growl.

"No," she states adamantly. "I did not start this charade, give up so much, to lose it all now."

The incredulous statement takes me by surprise. "To lose what? Your life? Your freedom? You've already lost one of those."

The expression on her gorgeous face hardens. "The power to survive. You may be able to quench your desires in battle, flit about the courts like a god, but there is no survival for me in this world without power, which I can only achieve through a *man*, of all things."

The bitter anger only makes me want her more. Gods, I have missed her ferociousness. Each cell screams for me to touch her, kiss her…but doing so here…in this place, would cause her nothing but harm.

"Then take *my* power. I'll give it to you freely."

She scoffs. The woman looks at me and *scoffs*. "You did not make such an offer on Dragobete."

"I would have," I state with complete conviction.

This time, her gaze lingers on me inquisitively, weighing my words. No doubt she can sense my truth. Then a sadness seeps into her eyes, and she turns away from me once more. "It's a pity you didn't."

"If I had…would you have spared me from the Datura Seeds?" I realize I am simply asking for her to wound me again, but I cannot hold back the question. Besides, even her wounds feel divine.

In slow, measured movements, as if still considering her answer, Luminita turns her head toward me. Those enigmatic blue eyes, fresh with unshed tears, find mine, and I can almost see the answer in their depths.

"Katharina!" A familiar voice summons every bit of my wrath, but Luminita's hand brushes mine.

"Don't," she whispers. "For both our sakes." Then she wipes her cheeks and plasters on a hollow smile that makes my stomach sink before turning toward her husband.

"Vlad," her head bows slightly, and the submissive act twists my insides. This goddess should not bow or cower to *anyone*, especially not a half breed brute like Vlad Dracul.

The young man's hostile glare is fixed on me instead of his blushing bride. "I relieve you of your *tedious* duty and retrieve *my wife*." The threat is rather blatant and bold, which only stirs my bloodlust more. I want to rip this man's throat from his dying corpse right here in the middle of court.

"I'm relieved," Luminita says while taking a step toward him, her palm resting on his chest. The touch draws the man's attention from me, and the look he gives my goddess makes my blood run cold–lust, jealousy, anger, and violence. "I'm rather tired after the long ride, and you know how I am with crowds."

"Well, then. You should rest!" John's boisterous voice shakes me from the rage-fueled trance. He strolls up behind Vlad, patting the bastard's shoulder. "My servants will show you to a room you may use for the night, but I insist you both join me and Bogdan for dinner."

My gaze snaps to John with a tilt of my head, but my friend ignores my obvious concern.

Vlad's dark gaze rakes over me before he turns back to Luminita. "The Voivode is right. You should rest." His gruff voice is flat without a hint of concern. In fact, I get the distinct impression malice lingers behind those words.

I want to tear her from his arms and take her away from this place, save her from this horrific fate she's brought upon herself, but Luminita is right about one thing. We are playing human games, and there is power in numbers. Times were simpler when men didn't have armies to command, and the world is a smaller place now.

9.   Something to Fear

Luminita

As soon as the door to our room closes and we are alone, Vlad storms up to me, snatching my arm. "Who is he?"

Although I expected the response, it still surprises me for some reason. Perhaps merely seeing Aaron has thrown me off entirely. Still, I manage to quickly pull on a confused frown. "Who?"

This only seems to infuriate him more. His grip tightens and violence rumbles beneath his skin, heralding the storm about to break. "Bogdan!" he snarls with a possessive scowl.

I'm unsure if it's because of Aaron and his words, or because I've had enough, but I yank my arm from his iron grip with a scathing glare. "I don't know what you mean, *husband*. I've only just met the man."

While Vlad stands still, a pillar of rage and darkness, I turn away and stroll toward the window. I don't get far. He catches me in a few quick strides and whirls me around to face him.

"Lies do not become you," he growls.

If he only knew. It's a struggle to keep the smug grin off my face. The man who thinks he owns me knows *nothing* about who I am. "You are paranoid…on edge because of where we are. I do not know the man."

Those blue-grey eyes harden. "Then why, dear wife, did he stare at you like he'd seen a ghost?"

I take a step forward with a stern frown, surprising him. "How am I to know the minds of men? Perhaps I remind him of someone. That is hardly *my* fault."

Vlad recovers quickly and grips my jaw, studying my eyes. "*You* seemed just as affected." The hold becomes painful as his fingers press into my skin.

All my instincts command that I rip away his essence until nothing remains, and I almost give in. But…if he were found here dead with only me, I would surely be hanged for his murder, and that is not something I would survive. The fact that I cannot even defend myself without risking my life sickens me to no end. I'd rather be hunted in the woods.

"You are hurting me, husband," I manage to say without allowing the threat to seep into my voice.

His grip softens, but just barely. "And you don't think your behavior hurt me?" Beneath the anger lies a vulnerability, a truth I am loath to admit. The brutal man does love me deeply in his way.

"I did not intend to hurt you," I say honestly. "I swear it."

The rage banks to embers, and he releases my jaw to brush his fingers over my cheek. I close my eyes and pull back the feel of Aaron's touch, which floods me with desire despite so much time apart. I feel my cheeks heat and my body tremble. Of course, Vlad believes it is all for him.

"Look at me, my love," he whispers softly, and I comply. "Swear to me."

A frown wrinkles my brow. "I *am* sworn to you, husband."

Tension fills his body, but he keeps his anger in check. "No. Swear to me you do not know Bogdan."

There is a split second where I am aware of how dangerous the lie is, but it leaves my mouth anyway. "I swear it."

When his lips crash against mine, the kiss is tender. A rare thing for him. I summon my memories of Dragobete and Aaron's devastating kiss, filled with such intense passion. I can feel the tears behind my closed eyelids as I pour everything I felt that night into this kiss. It feels wrong, like another betrayal of the one I care about, but I must sell the lie. I need Vlad to see nothing else but an enamored wife.

He breaks the kiss with a breathless whisper while cradling my face in his palms. "I love you, my wife."

"And I love you, husband." The lie twists my stomach, and the memory of Aaron's bracketed smile turns it from painful to agonizing.

"I need something from you," he whispers against my skin.

"What do you need?" I ask softly.

He nudges my lips with his and whispers, "Blood."

I instinctively pull away. "What?"

Vlad grabs my hand and pulls me back to him. "I did not feed before we left. I can feel the burning in my chest, the irritability, the paranoia. I need to feed."

"On me?" I ask incredulously. "You have never asked that."

Suspicion clouds his stormy eyes again. "I have never had need to." He studies my face with building anger. "I thought you liked my darkness."

"I do, but…"

"But not where you are concerned?" The question sounds like an accusation. An accurate one. "Katharina, we are guests in this court. I am trying to form a rapport with our host to repair damage. I cannot simply attack one of his people, even a servant. It would be seen as a violation of his hospitality."

Unfortunately, the man is correct, leaving me little choice. Still, I have no idea how he will react to my blood. In humans, it often heals wounds and sickness—one of the many reasons we remain so secretive. But to a strigoi?

Fingers drift into my hair, pulling me from my thoughts, and I focus on those intense blue-grey eyes.

"Katharina, I need this from you," he states plainly. "Do not make me force it from you."

Those words burn in my gut, and I can barely contain my rage. "Fine," is all I manage to say. I have not endured all this degradation only to have it go up in flames now.

Desire floods over my skin. He's wanted this for quite a while, and I'd been able to keep him at bay, but this time, he's forced my hand. I'm sure his choice not to feed before we left was intentional. He knew I'd have no choice.

While strangling my fury, I tilt my head and close my eyes. The bite where my neck meets my shoulder is not gentle. His teeth invade my flesh like swords, but I refuse to even give him the satisfaction of a whimper.

Vlad's arm tightens around my waist, pulling me tight against him, as euphoric lust tears through him. His teeth burrow deeper, and I can't hold back the muted sound of my discomfort.

I've watched him feed many times, but don't recall this reaction. Fear begins to wiggle into my thoughts, and when a wave of dizziness grips me, it turns to panic.

"Vlad. Stop." The words only emerge as a breathy plea.

His chest heaves against me while he withdraws his fangs from my neck with great reluctance. Then he crowds my vision with an enthralled grin. "Katharina." It's the passionate whisper of a lover possessed. "You…taste…" He searches my face as if never truly seeing me before. "Exquisite."

The rabid desire burning in his eyes terrifies me.

A frown suddenly pulls at his features, and he caresses my cheek. "Do not be scared of me, my love."

My love. The fact that he means those words only makes them more painful.

Vlad's hand falls from my face, and his frown deepens. "Why would my words cause you pain?"

I must have let my mask slip, distracted by the aching wound. "Not your words," I say softly while pulling away. My fingers slip over the bloody marks in my skin with a slight wince.

"I am sorry. I should have been gentler with you."

The rare apology captures my notice, and I peer at him. "I should lie down." I move to the bed and sink onto the mattress, truly exhausted. It isn't just the physical.

My thoughts drift to Aaron. He never even asked to bite me. Never broached the subject. Longing and regret consume my soul.

"What are you thinking about?" Something about his threatening tone disturbs me, but I'm unsure why.

"I'm merely tired," I reply, lying back on the bed.

Suddenly, he's on top of me, pinning my shoulders to the mattress. His turbulent eyes are full of rage, but why?

"Vlad. What is wrong?"

He merely stares at me like I'm an intricate puzzle.

Frustration burns through my veins. I'm weary of his games, but I pull on the concerned expression of a dutiful wife.

Vlad's eyes widen. "Why would you be frustrated with me, my love?"

Confusion sets in, but I don't let him see it. I know I play my part too well for him to make such accurate assumptions.

"Is the question confusing to you?"

Dread blossoms in my chest, and his expression hardens.

"What are you truly scared of?"

"Why do you ask, husband?" The question is shaky even to my ears.

Desire and anger heat his eyes in equal measure. "Because I feel it…as if it is my own."

For a moment, it feels as if my heart has stopped dead in my chest.

"What are you?" he asks in a feral growl.

"Your wife."

My answer only stokes his fury. "Your blood tastes like no other and now…I sense every flicker from you."

Pure panic sears my nerves, and I push at him, but he doesn't move. I try to push harder, using my unnatural strength, but still, he doesn't move.

"Why so eager to run away, little wife?" A vicious smile curves his lips, and he tears at my corset, ripping the delicate lace and silk.

Despite my best efforts, revulsion makes my throat tighten and tears fill my eyes.

Vlad flinches as if I've physically struck him. Then his eyes are on me again. "I repulse you?" The utter betrayal in his voice is horrifying.

"Vlad, no!" I insist, reining in as much of my chaotic emotions as I can, but white-hot panic still blares in the background.

"I'll give you something to fear, *my love*." He spits the title with heart-stopping fury and tears wildly at my dress like a man possessed.

I try to push him away from me, but it's as if he's suddenly composed of stone. Fear and panic overtake me, and I snatch hold of his wrist.

Vlad's violent glare snaps to mine, and I draw in his anger, pulling it from him. His hands still. He shakes his head. Then he pulls away, scrambling to his feet with an enraged stare.

"What did you do to me?" he snarls.

Panic still has me in its hold, my chest heaving for each labored breath.

"Answer me!" he demands, taking a small step forward.

"I…" the words die in my constricting throat, and my gaze falls to the floor.

Before I've even realized he's moved, pain erupts across my cheek from a forceful hit. "What did you do?" Each word is a vicious threat.

Tears well in my eyes, and I hate him for that. There is no point in hiding it now, so I let him see every last drop.

To my surprise, a laugh erupts from his throat, though it sounds wicked. "Katharina…" He draws in a deep breath, expanding his broad chest. "Such secrets." Vlad paces forward and bends to meet my hostile glare. "And Bogdan. Did you lie about him, too?"

Not even five hundred years of schooling my emotions could keep the fear of that question out of my mind.

Vlad hangs his head and draws up to his full height. "It seems we have much to discuss." His hands smooth down his stark black doublet embroidered with red dragons. "But…that will have to wait. I am expected at dinner."

My breath hitches. "*We* are expected," I correct him.

Another dark laugh emerges. "You are tired, my love, remember?" Vlad strolls toward the door, but peers over his shoulder before opening it. "Besides, your dress is ruined. I'm afraid I'll have to make apologies for you."

Before I manage to say another word, he disappears through the door, and I hear the lock click in place, sealing me inside. My entire body trembles. If Vlad has gained my abilities…my sense of others' emotions, my strength…Aaron is in grave danger, and it's my fault. It's all my fault.

10.　Politics

Aaron

My eyes snap anxiously to the door every time I hear a sound. Another servant bringing in a dish, nothing more. My pounding heart stills again, and I struggle to keep the disappointment off my face.

"Bogdan. What has you so rattled?" John asks, leaning back in his seat at the table's end.

"Nothing," I shake my head and pull on a pleasant smile.

John raises a bushy eyebrow and stares at me.

With a resigned sigh, I sit back and meet his questioning gaze. "I don't get a good feeling from this Vlad character."

A barely restrained laugh escapes him in a huff. "That much was rather obvious. Is there something else you wish to disclose?"

"No," I state simply, smoothing the cloth napkin over my lap.

"I apologize for keeping you waiting." The gruff voice draws my attention to the door with a rumble of animosity.

Vlad stands there alone, his venomous stare fixed solely on me.

"And where is your lovely wife?" John's jovial voice seems intrusive while Vlad and I stare each other down.

A muscle twitches in the man's cheek, almost making him smile, before his gaze shifts to John. "My sincere apologies for my wife's absence. She is not feeling well, I'm afraid."

"Oh dear. Does she require a healer?" The concern in John's voice is genuine. The man lost his wife to sickness some years ago.

"No." As his gaze moves back to me, hatred seethes in his eyes. "She has a rather *weak* constitution."

My hands curl around the arms of my chair until the knuckles turn stark white. The rage those words summon is nearly all-consuming. I should tear out his beating heart for such blasphemy.

A corner of the man's mouth lifts while he studies me, as if he knows what I'm thinking. "But you know that, don't you, Sir Bogdan?"

A slight chill trickles down my spine. "I don't understand your meaning," I keep the response simple in case he merely wants to goad me into confirming a suspicion.

Vlad peers down at the floor and clasps his hands behind his back before strolling to his seat at the dining table. Once he's seated, his eyes meet mine again. "That you've met my wife before."

"Have I?" Boredom seeps into my tone, and I force myself to relax my death grip on the chair. "If I have, I don't recall."

A servant places a bowl of stew in front of me, and I use it as an excuse to break eye contact with the man. Luminita would never tell Vlad about me. This has to be a trap, baiting me in hopes of a confession. I still feel his intense stare on me, however.

"John, you were telling me about your thoughts on our guest?" I prod my friend, hoping he will turn the conversation away from me.

"Yes." There is some hesitation in his voice, but he flashes Vlad a bright smile. "I do appreciate you coming all this way to discuss things."

"It was my pleasure to do so. I only seek what is best for my home."

"Yes, well. I'm certain you understand my concerns here. You and I have a rather complicated past."

Vlad's gaze shifts to me again. "Sometimes the past is simply that."

I don't rise to the obvious bait. As much as I would enjoy tearing this man apart, any action would only confirm his suspicion and put Luminita in harm's way.

"I suppose that is true," John states between bites of stew. "I did not support your father's decision, by the way. Handing you and Radu over to the Ottoman Empire like sacrificial lambs was rather barbaric."

"I thought you were fond of Barbarians."

Another rather obvious slight at my expense. Perhaps I'll simply count them up and return each one with a slice of my sword one day.

John's laugh is rather forced. "Yes! I suppose I am when it comes to war. What did your wife call my general? *Sălbatic.* Savage."

The name spoken in this particular context grates my nerves, even more so because it directs the attention back to me.

"I've been called worse things," I mutter before taking another bite.

A hearty laugh escapes John this time. "That you have, my friend. The Turks call him *Şeytan*, the devil."

"And are you? A devil?"

This time, I meet Vlad's stare with a curling grin. "Indeed, I am."

Although his eyes narrow, the faint movement in his throat makes my grin widen. I prop my elbows on the table and lean forward. "I've been slaughtering men far longer than you've been alive. You get a taste for it after a while. Not just claiming a life, but the absolute glory of dismembering the enemy, reducing them to a pile of tattered flesh, watching their blood soak the earth." I clear my throat, but the grin remains. "I'm sure you have some experience with that."

"Dear God, Bogdan!" John snaps. "This is not appropriate dinner conversation."

"It's quite all right, Voivode." An almost imperceptible tremor hides in Vlad's voice, and I savor each bit of it. "We are all men of war, are we not?"

I level Vlad with the callous stare I've perfected over thousands of years while running my tongue over my teeth. "Are we? Are you old enough to count as a *man* of war? You've been in…one battle? How did that go for you?"

The absolute rage turning the upstart's face red is divine.

"Bogdan! That is quite enough!" John has never spoken to me in such a sharp tone. It seems I may have pushed a boundary a bit too far. Pity.

Vlad shoves his chair back from the table and stands, his dark glare fixed on me. I don't meet his eyes. The child is beneath me. His tantrum doesn't deserve my attention.

"My apologies, Voivode. It seems I have lost my appetite."

"Nonsense. We can all be civil, can't we, Bogdan?"

I dip my head and take another bite of stew, leaving them to interpret my action however they see fit.

"It is getting late, and I should see to *my wife*. She isn't fond of being alone for too long."

That gets to me. I lower my spoon into the bowl and sit up tall with a stare sharp enough to cut glass. "I'm sure she's missed you in your absence." Even a deaf man could hear the sarcasm in my tone. I know I'll pay for it. John's irate expression tells me as much, but the slight slip in Vlad's grin is worth it.

The moment Vlad storms into the hall, John turns on me. "What in the name of all that's holy was that?"

I use my tongue to pick at a piece of meat stuck between my teeth. "I don't like the man."

"*The man* is a guest in my court, and you insulted him multiple times! What are you thinking?"

I shrug and take another bite of stew. "I'm a barbarian, John. Remember? I keep telling you I am not suited for the court."

A napkin flies across the table. "By God's bones! I fight to get you to say a single word at these dinners most nights, and tonight…*of all nights*, you cannot hold your tongue!"

I release a heavy sigh and sit back in my chair, already bored with the evening. Seeing Luminita was the only reason I didn't find a way out of the invitation.

"Is what Vlad inferred true? Do you know his wife?"

"No. I do not," I state honestly. Katharina is a hollow shell of the goddess I knew, but I *will* breathe new life into her. I will find a way.

"Then what is going on in your head? You have not been yourself since they arrived."

For a moment, I ponder just how to answer his question. Then I peer over at him. "Does it not bother you that a man of twenty-one years and no title expects us to hold him in the same regard as you? You've lived twice as long, fought and *won* dozens of battles, are the regent to Hungary and Voivode of Transylvania. His lack of respect and deference offends me."

John's jaw tightens. He knows me too well, but with such flattery, he's disinclined to call me out on the half-truth.

"Perhaps I should retire for the evening."

"Perhaps you should," John states firmly.

I grab a small loaf of bread before I stand and take a bite, catching John's eye. "You should stop trying to make a gentleman of me. We both know it's a useless endeavor."

The man's lips press into a firm line to keep from smiling. Ultimately, he fails. "Bogdan. You do keep life entertaining, even here at court."

"I do what I can," I say with a smirk.

11.　The Fool

Luminita

Alternating bouts of rage, shame, fear, and dread pulse beneath my skin as I tear off the ruined dress. A desperate need to escape this prison claws at my twisted stomach. For nearly five hundred years, control has been the one thing I value above all else, the one thing I put first, and now…it feels like a fantasy.

Vlad's reaction to my blood was beyond unexpected. I've never gifted it to anyone, but my mother had a soft spot for humans. I'd seen her give blood to them before, and they never inherited anything from the exchange but the healing quality. However, Vlad is no mere human.

I toss the pile of tattered lace and blue silk into the fireplace and watch the flames dance and lick across the delicate fabric, consuming it. It doesn't quell the fear or the imprint of Vlad's rage still clinging to my skin. Even with his suspicions, I doubt he will openly attack Aaron tonight, but I can't shake the sinking sensation in my gut.

Vlad has a purpose here. He wants to befriend Hunyadi, gain his trust. Making a move against the Voivode's second in command would only hinder his endeavor. But…love makes one do crazy things. Does his ravenous desire for the crown outweigh his poisoned love toward me? Impulse control is not a skill he's developed in his twenty-one years. The dress turning to ash is proof of that.

I turn away from the fireplace, still fighting the sickening feeling in my stomach, and glance down at the simple underdress. The fabric is thin…suggestive, similar to the shift I wore all those years ago…the one that summoned Aaron's desire.

Jenny Allen

A soft smirk curls my lips while I pace over to the pack with my traveling clothes. The shift did not summon Sălbatic's desire. It didn't matter what I wore—a shift, a ritual dress, a gown of silk and lace, nothing at all… After all this time…after everything that transpired between us, he *still* desires me with the same fervor he displayed that night.

His last question still haunts me. If he'd offered me control and power, if he fell willingly at my feet, would I have saved him from the Datura seeds? I wanted to say yes, but…Aaron is dangerous in a way Vlad is not.

My husband may have the upper hand right now, but I still know who I am. I can remain true to myself. I can seize control if necessary.

With Aaron…my desire to be lost in him is overwhelming. Even if he laid all the control at my feet, I'd forget I wanted it. I would lose sight of the things I crave. That's why I panicked and forced him to drink the poisoned wine—to save my soul from being seduced, from drowning in him.

I pull on a wool dress of simple grey and let the warmth seep into my skin, allowing it to become my armor. My fingers drift absently over my hand where the imprint of Aaron's desire still lingers. It calms my racing heart, providing an odd comfort, and that disturbs me.

I should sneak out, take my horse, and run. The most logical solution is to escape the violent man I'm tied to and the passionate one who would dominate my heart regardless of his intentions. But they would both hunt me, and the world has become a smaller place.

No. I straighten and smooth the lines of my dress with determination. I will not run. I will not give Vlad that satisfaction. He knows I am different now…something other. Perhaps I should show him just how *different* I am.

The man may have my strength and my ability to sense emotion, but he will *still* underestimate me because of my gender.

I snatch the dagger from his things and storm over to the door. After placing my back to the wall beside it, I close my eyes and stuff every emotion into that deep, dark pit in my mind. I work slowly and methodically as I had in my youth when hiding from the other Durand until my mind is silent, and I wait.

The lock clicks, and my eyes gradually open. I keep everything suppressed, giving Vlad nothing to sense. The door swings open, and heavy boots stomp against the floor. I move swiftly, snatching Vlad's throat and shoving him against the wall while kicking the door closed. The dagger is at his throat before his stormy eyes focus on my face.

Rage and shock flares beneath my palm, but my fingers tighten as I hold his narrowed stare.

"I told you," I spit through gritted teeth. "If you strike me, it will be the last thing you do." I press the blade tighter to his throat with just enough pressure to break the skin.

The curled lip beneath his moustache twitches, but he doesn't dare speak and risk slitting his own throat.

"You wanted to know who I am?" I lean a little closer, letting the hate leak from my emotional pit. "I am a goddess of righteous fury, and *you* have angered me."

The wrath I expect, but the flood of lust takes me by surprise. He grabs my wrist, firmly but not painfully so, and moves the dagger away from his throat enough to speak.

"I believe you, Katharina. Do you wish to kill me? To die together?"

The truth of his words further twists my stomach. Taking his life would result in me losing mine as well, especially here. Aaron may be the Voivode's second in command, but not even he could save me from that fate, and Vlad knows it.

"I don't have to kill you, *husband*." I latch hold of his essence and rip enough to put the vile man on his knees. "I simply need to teach you the proper way to worship," I hiss while his eyes widen.

"What witchcraft do you wield?" The question emerges with a tremble that swims through my blood hypnotically.

I lean close, my piercing stare boring into him. "You've had but a taste of my power. I am no more a witch than you are, Vlad. We are simply two creatures who exist above humans. Expose me, and I will share every one of your bloody secrets and let these people hunt you like the animal you are."

"Why would I expose you when I have you all to myself? I *own* a goddess." The reverent words summon my wrath, and I draw more from his essence.

"You *own* nothing!"

Vlad recovers quicker than expected. He knocks the blade from my hand, grabs my hips, and pulls me violently to my knees. It has to be my blood…

Before the thought fully registers, his hand is twisted in my hair, holding me close to him. "*You are mine*," he snarls possessively before claiming my mouth.

I push at his chest with that sickening sensation rising once more, but his other arm clamps around me. His teeth nip my lip, drawing blood, and I use all my strength to tear my mouth away from his.

A decadent sigh rushes past his lips, coating my skin. "By the gods, you are delicious." His fingers tighten in my hair, pulling my head back, and his blue-grey eyes fix on me. "Has Bogdan tasted you? Is that why he seethes with hatred and jealousy?"

I go still, shock tearing through each fiber of my being. "I don't know what you mean."

The corner of his mouth lifts in a dark grin full of deadly promises. "You know precisely what I mean. He shares the same hunger…older, but I recognized it. Has he tasted you?"

I barely manage to swallow past the fear cinching my throat.

That dark glare sharpens, and he pulls my face closer until our lips almost touch. "Answer me," he demands in slow, sharp tones.

"No." The word escapes in a breathy whisper, and he seems to sense the truth of it.

"Then why does he desire you so much?"

As if my blood is my only worth. "You would not understand," I state with as much venom as I feel.

"And why is that, my wife?"

Rage and fear roar through my body, stealing my cold logic. In this moment, I only want to inflict pain. "Because you do not understand what love is."

Terrifying wrath slams against me like a physical blow, and I immediately regret the words.

"Love?" he growls, fingers tightening until the pain in my scalp is sharp. "You love him?"

I don't allow myself time to think. "No. *He* loves *me*. I am not capable of such a thing." The words leave a bitter taste in my mouth, but I give him nothing to sense.

Those blue-grey eyes sharpen to points. "My dear wife. I do believe you are lying to me."

"I am not!" I shout with a hateful glare.

"Then you won't care when I kill him."

I laugh with every shred of animosity I can muster. "You are a fool."

Draga & the Savage: Dracul

"Am I?" He studies me, but I latch onto that dark humor, wrapping it around everything else. "Perhaps I'll merely expose him for what he is."

Despite all my efforts, the threat strikes true. "Do that and I will destroy you."

Vlad's teeth scrape over his lip, and he grins like a demon. "Then we all die, but he won't have you."

"You wouldn't risk your precious crown." Even as the words leave my mouth, I know now they are untrue. Vlad is a strigoi obsessed, and my heart sinks into the pit of my stomach.

"I would." The sinister whisper makes me tremble. "Hmm," he muses with delight. "You will leave with me at first light. We will return home, and you *will* be a dutiful wife." His sickening gaze rakes over me hungrily before pausing on the curve of my neck. His fingertips trace the unblemished skin where he'd bitten me earlier. "More surprises."

He bends closer, mouth hovering over the spot, but I snatch his throat and shove him back. "No!"

His threatening glare shifts to my eyes from beneath his heavy brow. "Your duty as my wife is to give me what I need."

"You don't *need* it."

The man smirks. "Fine. To give me what I *want*."

"And if I refuse?"

Vlad's grin widens. "I believe you know my answer. Bogdan."

Violent panic tightens my chest, and I swallow hard. He means every word. Comply, or Bogdan suffers, and both Vlad and I will follow. I'm uncertain whether my hand leaves his throat because of concern for Aaron or myself. Or perhaps, I'm simply too scared to admit the truth vibrating in my bones. *Prostul moare de grija alutia*—The fool dies worrying about someone else.

Tonight, as his teeth sink viciously into my skin, I am the fool.

12. Gone

Aaron

A knock on my door wakes me from nightmares of Vlad taking his anger out on Luminita. I groan and squint at the late morning sun invading my room. I should have checked on her, stopped Vlad, killed the bastard, but I realize none of those were viable options last night, as much as it pains me.

After so much time, she's right here…in this building, and I can't even summon a legitimate reason to see her. Any move I make, especially after my behavior at dinner, would cause her harm, and she is quite literally the last person on this miserable earth I want to see harmed. Gods. She was an absolute vision in that dress…the blue silk making her luminous eyes glow against her porcelain skin.

The knock is louder this time, more insistent.

With an aggravated growl, I shove out of bed and stalk to the door. I don't bother with a shirt. The trousers make me decent enough to yell at whoever is knocking. When I rip open the door, I'm greeted by the shocked face of a familiar young boy.

"What do you want?" The menace in my voice only makes the child's eyes widen more. "Speak!"

"The…uh. Voivode Hunyadi wishes to see you, sir. Right away." As soon as the boy rattles off the summons, he darts down the hall. At least I still have the ability to frighten small children.

My thoughts immediately return to Vlad, and I slam the door closed. The man is quick to anger, but not quick to fear, unfortunately.

There must be a solution to this maddening dilemma. Luminita doesn't love him. I saw it in her eyes, those enigmatic blue eyes wet with tears. I'm afraid Vlad might know it, too, after last night.

His comments hit too close to home. He knows something about us. Luminita would never tell him, but he's obviously pieced it together somehow. Although my stunned reaction to seeing her probably began the train of thought. The woman does have a certain effect on me. She always has.

I rub a hand over my face and sigh heavily before tugging on my shirt. I make quick work of the belt, socks, and boots while my mind continues to work the problem. It's infuriating. I am an ancient god, and Luminita is the goddess of blood and chaos, yet we are forced to cower to the rules of *human men*. Perhaps I should form my own army and wipe their threat from the earth. A rather impractical thought since I require their blood to survive.

As I march back toward the door, something occurs to me. After last night, an early morning summons from John might include Vlad. He most likely wants to smooth things over. Unfortunately, I did not wake up choosing peace. Actually, I *never* wake up choosing peace. War is in my blood. I'll choose violence every time.

Well, there's no sense in delaying the inevitable. My time here had to come to an end eventually. If it doesn't result in a noose around my neck, I'll be fine without the pompous court politics.

The halls are quiet this morning except for the scuttling feet of maids and servants. My eyes linger on each closed door I pass, wondering which one she hides behind. To think that a few inches of wood stand between me and my goddess is beyond maddening. Mundane people…mundane objects…keeping us apart. It's unnatural.

The pull I feel in her presence, the one that draws me to her and crackles with life around us…it's just as potent as it was on Dragobete, and I know she feels it. She must. When I asked her if she'd have spared me from the Datura Seeds…she wanted to say yes, *would have said yes*, if not for Vlad's arrival.

Once again, my jaw clenches painfully tight. Vlad Dracul the third. I don't often *hate* humans. The concept simply doesn't occur to me often. It's rather like hating a cow or a sheep. But Vlad…*that man*…I would *greatly* enjoy his suffering. Perhaps it's because he isn't human, or at least not entirely, according to Luminita.

It's been quite a while since I've crossed paths with another vampire. The last one was near the Serbian border. I met Vlad's father a time or two, but never got *that* impression. Of course, there is no way to tell by physical appearance alone without prying a person's mouth open and looking for fangs. That is not something one can accomplish in a public setting.

I halt outside John's door and listen for a moment. Pacing footsteps are all I hear, no voices. With a slow exhale, I raise my hand and rap my knuckles against the wood.

"Come in!" The shout doesn't sound friendly today.

Thankfully, when I open the Voivode's door, only John is present. At least one thing has gone right so far.

"How can I be of assistance, John?"

The man peers up at me from beneath a heavy brow. "Vlad left early this morning."

The news makes my entire body go still, and I swallow hard. "Vlad and his wife?"

John's brow furrows. "Yes, of course."

She's gone. Two hundred years, and I had mere *moments* with her. The knowledge twists my insides into agonizing knots until I feel like retching.

The Voivode sighs heavily and slouches in his chair. "The next time they come to court, you will behave yourself, or I'll have no choice but to ban you. Am I understood?"

"Why do you care what that violent boy thinks?" I ask, unable to stop myself.

"The boyar families are pushing for someone to replace Vladislav, and right now, Vlad Dracul is my only viable option. Your opinion of the man has no place in politics. And if there is *any* validity to Vlad's claim that you *know* his wife, you had better play nice for *her* sake."

I nod somberly. The man is right. Riling Vlad might have been fun, but Luminita likely paid the price. I should mount up right now and chase after them, tear her free of him. But my little display last night at dinner solidified my position as the man's enemy. If he were to die right now, John would suspect only me, and it would confirm Vlad's claims about Luminita. Of all the things humans invented over the years, politics is by far my least favorite.

"Is there any truth to it?" John implores with an almost sympathetic look.

"No," I state adamantly. Any other answer would mark her as a harlot. "She reminds me of someone I lost." At least this part is honest. "And I don't care for the way he treats her."

Another heavy sigh escapes my friend. "She is *his* wife, Bogdan. As much as you may dislike how he treats her, there is no law against it."

"There should be," I growl.

"In the eyes of God, she is *his* property to do with as he pleases. Her role is to merely be obedient. Who are we to argue with God?"

I turn an irate glare on my friend. "A god created by mortal men to justify their actions."

John's eyes narrow. "Careful, Bogdan. You may be my friend, but blasphemy is a serious crime. Besides, you take advantage of the scripture, doling out justice in barbaric fashion."

And she deserves justice, I think to myself.

"Bogdan. I understand how memories can haunt us. I even understand your concern for Lady Dracul. I never raised a hand to Elizabeth. She gave me Ladislaus and Matthias, two perfect boys, before the Lord took her from me too soon. But you cannot afford to make him an enemy."

I scoff. "The man has already made *me* his enemy. He hurled accusations the moment he set foot in the room last night."

John's gaze falls to the floor with a huff. "Let me remind you that *you* are the one who refuses a title, and because of that, you haven't a leg to stand on here. You are merely my general. Vlad is of noble birth. Any slight against you won't matter. Short of physically attacking you in front of me, I cannot help you."

I press my lips into a firm line to keep the smile from my face. I'm uncertain whether John said the last bit out of frustration or to help me, but he's given me a plan.

A year and a half passes before Vlad Dracul appears at court again... alone. My mind immediately races to dark thoughts of Luminita's fate. Fortunately, John decides not to test my self-control. He whisks the man into talks, shares a private dinner, and then sends him on his way the next morning.

I did receive a letter from John after Vlad's departure.

Bogdan,

I did inquire after the Lady Dracul. She was unwell and did not desire to travel. Vlad assured me she will be fine and will accompany him on his next visit. I hope this puts your mind at ease, my friend.

-John

I crumple the aggravating letter into a ball and toss it in the fire. Vlad could claim whatever he likes. There is no one to hold him responsible. But if Luminita is not with him on his next visit, I will ride for the Suceava court and see her for myself. If anything has befallen her…I *will* hold Vlad responsible…in every painful way I can imagine, and I've had *thousands of years* to imagine.

13. Will of God

Luminita
Suceava – March 1453

With the five-day ride to Beszterce, a day or two at court, and another five days back to Suceava, I have at least eleven days of freedom, perhaps twelve. Vlad was less than thrilled when I refused to accompany him, but since I've been so *weak* lately, he did not push the issue.

As much as I loathe the deception, feigning exhaustion, applying dark colors below my eyes, allowing *a man* to believe he has broken me…it is the only way to keep him from feeding on me regularly. I do not wish Aaron to start a war by tearing Vlad to shreds, as much as I'd love to witness it.

Beyond that, I do not want Aaron to see me stoop to such tactics… debasing myself in such a fashion, especially after all I sacrificed to avoid a fate exactly like this one.

After washing my face in the basin, I pace to the window and peer over the buildings and gardens of Suceava, glowing orange with the setting sun. Things were so simple once.

Memories of the market at Deva drift back to me. The sunset glowed over the vendors when we arrived that evening, lighting the place with oranges and reds like it does now. We were little more than traveling companions in that moment.

Then I recall the crowd pushing us together, my body trapped between Aaron and the wall…his intense grey eyes filled with such lustful passion…the word he accidentally uttered…*Draga*…beloved. Perhaps we were more even then.

Regardless, we were both free. Humans had no say in our lives. We moved about the world, revered, feared, worshipped like the deities we were. And now...

Cold seeps into my bones, and I wrap my arms around myself. Tears fill my eyes. I allow it only because I'm alone, and Vlad is not here to witness them. I refuse to give him that satisfaction.

Once every moon cycle, Vlad takes my blood. He's more demanding of my body in the days following. I can't tell if he simply craves the feel of my disgust and hatred, or if he's testing to see if those emotions have changed. The one small mercy is that the effects from my blood are not permanent.

For roughly three days, he is stronger, heals faster, and can sense emotion. Thank the gods he hasn't figured out how to draw the essence from people. Perhaps he can't. Maybe that is a skill only the Durand can wield. If I survive this hell I've brought upon myself, I shall have to test my theories.

Vlad, of course, demanded my blood before leaving for Beszterce, to test Aaron further, no doubt, but my ruse worked well. Killing Vlad is not an option so long as he's favored for the crown of Wallachia. But making him believe my life is at risk...that he may lose the object of his twisted obsession, gives him pause, and he left for the Voivode's court without feeding on me.

It's not simply my blood he craves, though. He wants an heir, a union of our unique bloodlines. More disturbingly, Vlad wants my love, as if I'd *ever* grant him my heart. It belongs to *no one, especially not Vlad.*

The madman does not see his actions as sins. He is merely a *devoted* husband, punishing me for my wickedness and taking what is rightfully his in the eyes of the law. A law created by the infernal Roman Catholic Church, which he claims to detest. He still does not comprehend the flaws in his logic. Of course, most men don't. They pick and choose which principles fit them best and ignore the rest of the dogma.

Vlad truly believes that one day, after bedding me against my will in violent fashion every other night and forcefully drinking from me, I will simply forget my disgust and love him. Delusional does not come close to an accurate portrayal of his mind.

So many times, I've wanted to consume enough of his essence to make him pass out while he pumps into me like a wild beast, but his threat constantly echoes in my head. If I do not play the part of a *dutiful* wife, he will reveal Aaron, putting his life in danger.

Draga & the Savage: Dracul

Despite the lesson I learned from my father's demise, I suffer to prevent the destruction of another. *Prostul moare de grija alutia*—The fool dies worrying about someone else. Perhaps that is the inevitable fate of my family, a curse we all bear.

It is yet another reason I did not wish to travel to Beszterce. Aaron cannot know why I endure this fate for two reasons. The knowledge would provide Aaron with further motivation to tear Vlad apart, and even if he succeeded, it would still result in Aaron's death.

The second reason…

I sigh and rest my temple against the cool stone wall. Admitting it out loud, especially to Aaron, means facing truths I do not have the strength to confront. As long as the knowledge is mine alone, I can rationalize my actions. It is nothing more than my desire to prevent the destruction of a unique specimen who has survived thousands of years. It has nothing to do with the convoluted mess of emotions growling and snapping in the depths of the pit I've sequestered them to.

I cannot open the pit. Too much lives there now. Most of it is darkness. The only solution is to feel nothing, to give Vlad nothing to sense, to crush any hope Aaron has that I am capable of love. I realize the latter is the most difficult of those tasks.

Tears fill my eyes once more at the mere thought, despite keeping a supposedly tight lid on the pit. Apparently, one emotion is more difficult to wrangle and eradicate than others—despair.

The world of men is a cruel place, and it seems to worsen with every generation. The only comfort is knowing that once Vlad is in power, I will finally have a voice. The wife of the Prince of Wallachia can accomplish a great number of things, but…

Melancholy finds me again. I must produce an heir, and Vlad will still have legal dominion over me.

I thought aligning myself with a strigoi would work to my benefit. I thought he'd relentlessly pursue the crown in ruthless battles, and perhaps he will. But I did not consider his ruthlessness with me. After all, Aaron treated me fairly, even after I betrayed him, and he is more strigoi than Vlad. Age could be the difference, or perhaps the human part of Vlad is responsible for his wickedness. I refuse to acknowledge that it just as easily could be because Aaron loves me.

"Lady Dracul?" An old woman's voice shakes me from my troubled thoughts, and I turn toward the door to see my favorite servant of the court.

Antonia comes from an old Dacian line of herb workers. She has many connections and can get almost anything with enough time and money. I have given her more than enough of both.

"Antonia, come in." The warm smile stretching my lips is genuine. "Did you get what I requested?"

The woman's dark eyes shift about nervously before she closes the door. "Yes, m'lady," she says in a conspiratorial whisper. The woman shuffles toward me, gaze casting about as if we may not be alone. Then she reaches into the large pouch hanging from her waist. "The items you requested."

Her voice lowers further as she withdraws a package. "Atropa Belladonna, Salvia, Mandrake, and…"

When she hesitates, a vicious sense of reliving a memory steals my breath. There was a moment at a vending booth in Deva where I spoke with another old woman about forbidden items.

"Datura seeds," she barely whispers.

"How many?" I ask. The seeds are the most potent and can be difficult to find these days. Their use as a powerful hypnotic and a deadly poison in high doses has made even the herb itself scarce.

Antonia's stare fixes on me. "These are very dangerous herbs. If anyone knew—"

"No one will know unless *you* tell them," I interrupt with a thinly veiled threat.

The wrinkles on the old woman's brow deepen. "I would be found just as guilty for procuring them."

I nod and set the package on the table to unwrap it. "Then we have an understanding. There are several ducats on the table beside the door."

The woman snatches the coins before she hurries out of the room, most likely eager to be away from the contraband.

A small pouch rests atop the other herbs in the unwrapped bundle. There is no heaviness in my heart when I pick up the bag. There is no confliction when I tip the Datura seeds into my palm. There is no apprehension when I stare down at the seeds, which resemble tiny river stones. After all, *these* are not for Aaron this time.

If Vlad were to suffer a sudden death, it would put my life at risk. But a slow descent into madness, a sickness drawn out over time… I cannot be blamed for the ways of nature and the will of God.

14. Heaven

Aaron
Beszterce Court – July 1453

Each nerve itches as I pace back and forth on the dais. Vlad is due to arrive today, and John insisted I be present and make a *friendly* impression. Rumors are circulating about a potential threat to Belgrade, and John wants to include Vlad in our plans. His metal must be tested in true battle, he'd said.

Every cell of my body rebels at the very thought. However… Luminita is due to arrive with him, and it's been two years since I've laid eyes on her. A miserable two years that have felt more like a millennium or two, which is a concept I fully comprehend after enduring over seven of them.

The doors open, and I stop, my head snapping up. But when a few men stroll in, laughing, a growl escapes my throat.

"Bogdan. Sit!" John snaps. "You're pacing like a caged animal."

"Because I am one. I don't belong here, John, and I have little desire to conspire with Vlad Dracul."

John's eyes narrow on me. It's not the first time he's been suspicious of me and my connection to Vlad's wife, Katharina. I suppose the effect she has on me is rather obvious. She is far more skilled at acting unaffected. Unless…she truly is unaffected. I dismiss the stomach-churning thought with another growl.

No. The tears in her eyes were genuine, the thick tension drawing us together, the way her breaths quicken when I'm close… I am not the only one who feels it.

"Bogdan! Sit!" John repeats in a firmer tone that grates my already fraying nerves.

I comply, because if I don't, he'll toss me out of court. I could miss my chance to see her, and my eyes are starving for her. Not only my eyes, but…all things in good time.

"If you can manage some semblance of civility, I'll grant you a reprieve. I'll discuss the basic matters with Vlad alone, but I will send for you once I've relayed all the pertinent information. You, me, and Vlad will need to plan together."

I stretch my neck with a heavy sigh. "If my presence is necessary, then I am at your service, Voivode Hunyadi."

John cracks a genuine smile. "Don't sound so overjoyed, Bogdan."

I lean forward to rest my elbows on my knees and peer at him from beneath my brow. "I am at your service. My happiness is *not* a requirement. You know my feelings on this subject."

The smile dims until John nods with a somber expression. "That is fair, my friend. Shake the man's hand, be polite, don't gawk at his wife, and you'll be free for a few hours before I need you again. Agreed?"

"Agreed," I say begrudgingly. Any amount of time spent in Vlad's presence is a torment I'd rather avoid, but human politics demands it. For what feels like the millionth time in the past few years, I curse the wretched creatures who created this dance of lies.

The doors swing open again, and my entire body tenses in the chair like a string pulled taut. Somehow, I know it's her about to enter. My body reacts without even seeing her.

Vlad's boots come into view first, immediately summoning a deep pit of animosity, but I keep my face neutral. Skirts of greenish blue swish past the door, then I see her arm looped through his, the delicate curve of her neck, the raven-black curls drawn up due to the summer heat, and finally…her down-turned face.

There is something haunting about the way her gaze never lifts from the floor as they approach the dais. In fact, her movements seem…unlifelike, as if she is merely going through the motions required of her. And I realize that is precisely what we are both doing in this moment.

Still…seeing my vengeful goddess like this…seemingly broken…tears my heart to shreds even before her vacant gaze lifts. A polite smile curves her lips, but she looks straight ahead at no one in particular, playing a part.

I rub a hand over my face to prevent tears from stinging my eyes and stand.

"Ah, the Lady Dracul. Such a vision as always!" John exclaims in a boisterous voice.

Luminita's gaze moves to him, and her smile brightens a touch. "Lovely to see you again, Voivode." Even her voice sounds wooden and distant.

For a brief second, her gaze cuts in my direction, but never comes close to meeting mine. "General Bogdan." There is no warmth in the greeting, but her chest rises and falls a little faster.

I straighten, swallowing down the bitter hatred I have for Vlad and what he's reduced Luminita to. With calm purpose, I stride up to the Lord Dracul and extend my hand, even though it sickens me. "My apologies for how we left things on our last meeting." Forcing those vile words from my lips tests my patience.

Luminita was the first person to force a polite request or an apology from my lips. The woman taught me the true value of one singular moment. She is the addiction from which I will *never* recover. And apologizing to her tormentor is a fresh level of hell I am not eager to experience again.

Vlad's dark stare lingers on my hand before he defiantly meets my eyes. He makes it perfectly clear we are *not* friends, a fact I wholeheartedly agree with, but John expects more from me.

"I hope we can plan together for the upcoming...issues, at least." Perhaps the temptation of war and power will sway him enough to get John off my back.

"Indeed," Vlad says brusquely while shaking my hand. I squeeze a little harder than necessary, enjoying the slight clench of his jaw. My willingness to play nice does have limits.

"Husband, I am rather tired from the ride." Luminita pats his arm, drawing his attention away from me.

"And I should check on that issue with the guards, Voivode. I'll await your summons. Lord and Lady Dracul." I bow, toss John a forced smile, and stalk out of the court.

A hundred emotions rampage through my mind like Turkish devils and contort my stomach into knots. All I can see is red as my boots march forward without a destination. She couldn't even bring herself to look at me.

My leg bumps into something, almost making me lose my balance.

"Sorry, Sir!" The boy exclaims in a terrified squeak.

I snatch him by the collar before he can scamper off.

"I'm truly sorry!" the thing pleads, which only furthers my irritation.

"Be silent!" I snap, and the boy goes still, wide eyes blinking up at me in terror.

I can't help but sigh in aggravation as I release him. "I have a task for you."

The fear lessens a bit.

"There's a florin in it for you if you're extra sneaky."

A bright smile cracks the boy's scared expression, and his big eyes shine. At least he appreciates a challenge.

"Do you know the Lord and Lady Dracul? They just arrived."

He nods.

"Good. Find out which room they are staying in, but don't let anyone know your mission or that *I* tasked you with it. Understood?"

The boy nods eagerly, his smile widening.

"Find me in the garden when you've accomplished your task."

"Yes, Sir!" he says excitedly before running off.

I cast one last glance at the open court doors before making my way out to the gardens.

I pace the same path for over half an hour, fingers brushing over the soft petals of red peonies, white carnations, yellow tulips, white martagon lilies, and plum irises. They are all soft things of beauty, but none of them compare…not to *her*.

When the boy finally appears, he hurries past the sculpted landscape in an all-out run and comes to a stop before me, chest heaving for breath. "I found…what you wanted…Sir. They have…the third quarters…down the east hall…on the right."

A smile tugs at my lips. "And you followed them there?"

"Yes, Sir," The boy nods, still gulping air. "Lord Dracul is meant to meet the Voivode soon. I'm supposed to issue him the summons."

The smile breaks free, stretching my lips, and I pat the boy's head. "Well done. You can deliver his summons now." I drop a gold florin in his palm, and the boy's eyes open impossibly wide.

"Thank you, Sir!"

This time, when he runs off, I follow. I keep a fair distance at a hurried pace, but don't allow him out of my sight. When he reaches their door and knocks, I duck into an alcove. Words are exchanged, and then Vlad's heavy boots march closer. I only catch a glimpse of his stern face, but it's enough to dredge up that deep well of seething hatred.

I wait until Vlad is far enough away that I can no longer hear the echo of his footsteps before sneaking down the hall toward their room.

Once I'm in front of the door, my heart thuds violently against my ribs, and I peer up and down the hall to ensure there's no one around. The longer I stand here, the more danger I put us both in. There is *no* logical or socially acceptable reason for me to be here. I raise my hand and knock.

Suddenly, the memory of standing outside our room at the inn in Deva flashes through my mind. The morning after the event that drove us apart, I had still gone back for her. I stood outside that door, knocking just as I do now, with the same hope and dread.

My thumb rubs absently over the small object sewn into my shirt's cuff. It typically brings me comfort, but in this moment, it only sharpens my anxiety.

Soft footsteps approach the door, and my blood rampages in my veins. The handle turns, and it feels like I can't breathe. The door opens, and the moment her luminous eyes meet mine, I am lost all over again.

I don't give her a chance to send me away or even speak. My hands move quickly, cradling her face, and my lips crash against hers in a desperate need to breathe life into her.

She's stunned, and I take advantage of it to back her up and kick the door closed. The sound breaks her shock, and she flings her arms around my neck, tongue meeting mine with a passionate moan. It absolutely breaks me. That fiery connection between us pulls taut. My hands surge down her simple underdress to grip her thighs, and I haul her up with ease.

Luminita's fingers dig into my hair, and she kisses me like a woman possessed, starved and ravenous. Each hypnotic move of her tongue drives me wild. I spin, putting her back to the wall, trapping her against me.

Another heady moan vibrates into our feral kiss, making my already hard cock throb painfully. The things this woman does to me…what no one has *ever* done to me…before or since…

Her hips move against mine, and I tug at the strings tying the top of her dress closed with an undeniable ache to feel her soft skin. The tie falls loose. Her breath hitches as my rough hand grabs her breast, rubbing against her pebbled nipple.

She breaks the kiss with a wild cry, arching into my touch, desperate for it. "Sălbatic," she says in a breathy whisper, setting my soul on fire once again.

My hand slides into her hair, drawing her mouth back to mine. Her lips part invitingly, and her tongue teases across my lip. I claim every inch of her mouth while her body writhes against me, hungry for friction.

When my head starts to spin, I break the kiss and try to drag in a few deep breaths. "Gods," I groan, my eyes finding hers. "I have missed you, *Draga mea.*" I can hear the tears in my voice, but to see them reflected in her eyes is the most exquisite sight.

"Kiss me, *Sălbatic meu,*" she whispers with a vulnerability I have not witnessed from her since that dreaded morning after Dragobete.

I obey the command of my goddess. My hand cradles her nape, and I capture her full lips in a scorching kiss. She grinds against me, once more seeking release, and I'm more than happy to help.

My hand slips beneath her dress and glides up her thigh. She breaks the kiss again, panting for breath, when my fingers find her heat, soaked with desire. She rocks wantonly against my fingers, her erotic moans growing louder. When I capture her mouth this time, it's to swallow the salacious sounds. I don't want anyone to hear, and they belong *only* to me.

No one can truly *own* Luminita, a fact Vlad will learn eventually. But I can own the sounds of her pleasure. Those I can claim with certainty.

Her breath hitches again when I sink two fingers inside, and my cock is instantly jealous. I've never believed in heaven, but I think I've found it regardless. My thumb and fingers continue to work her, driving her pleasure.

Luminita rips her mouth away from mine, gasping for air. Her walls start to pulse around my fingers, tension coiling through her body.

I was wrong. *This…* this moment right before she shatters…hovering on the edge of an abyss…*this* is heaven.

The moment my lips coast over her neck, her entire body clenches tight around me.

"No!" The terrified shriek is startling and not at all what I expect.

15.   Monster

Luminita

The moment I open the door and my gaze collides with Aaron's, a torrential wave of boundless, passionate *need* hits me. Before I can even catch my breath, his mouth crashes against mine and we're moving backward. The door slams closed, sealing us inside, cutting us off from the rest of the world, and I surrender.

I am so tired of fighting, struggling for a meager existence. For once, I just want to *feel*…to know I am still alive, that the sacrifices have not broken me, to be lost in a sea of unspeakable desire.

And gods…Aaron brings that out in me and so much more. The fear never even has a chance to take root. It's lost to the swell of primal longing…the gathering crescendo in my heart. I cling to him, lost, but every touch is vivid, infusing me with the carnal energy always pulsing between us.

I have *never* felt its equal. Not even close. The knowledge should scare me, terrify me, but when his fingers move inside me, working me toward the edge of euphoria, it leaves room for nothing else. It's all-consuming, making my head spin while I pant and moan his name…the one I gave him.

I hover on the edge…so close to coming undone and being lost to him forever.

Aaron's mouth skims over my neck and icy panic seizes my body. "No!" As soon as the strangled cry passes my lips, I can't breathe. My chest constricts, pain flares through me, and the panic only worsens.

I shove frantically at his chest. Confusion and heartache greet my touch, and it's *too much*.

He takes a step back, giving me space, and I scramble away from him, fighting to drag in air.

"Luminita? What is wrong?"

Tears flood my eyes. I can't think, can't stop shaking, can't stop feeling the horrid imprint of Vlad's teeth buried in my neck. My legs give out, and I sink to the floor.

Aaron is instantly there, cradling my face in his palms. "What happened? What did I do?"

The deep well of emotion in his touch makes my throat constrict, leaving me unable to utter a single sound.

"Talk to me," he pleads, and I want to.

Gods, I want to tell him everything, fall into his arms, and let the world disappear.

"Luminita, *Draga mea.*" Tears shine in his silvery eyes before he presses his forehead to mine, just like he did the morning after the ritual...after I betrayed him.

My heart fractures. *This* is why he is so dangerous. The power he has over me...if he has my blood, he'll know. I gather every scrap of strength I still possess and pull away from him. I can't tell if the grief I feel is mine or his. It is most likely both.

"You need to leave." I barely force the words past my lips. His confusion and pain are too much, so I rise to my feet and turn away, arms wrapping around myself.

Only seconds pass before I feel Aaron's warmth at my back. His hands gently wrap around my shoulders, and he leans into my hair. "Don't," he whispers, voice thick with tears. "Don't pull away again. Don't shut me out."

I squeeze my eyes shut against the burning tears and try to draw in a deep breath around the agony tearing at my chest. "I am *not yours* to do with as you please," the lie passes my lips with practiced ease, but I feel the fractures deepen.

The first flicker of anger reaches me, but doesn't last long. "That's not what this is, and you know it."

He's right. I do. But he is a strigoi...more powerful than Vlad. He craves blood.

Vlad was a possessive man with a rough streak when I met him, but the moment he tasted my blood, he became a monster—vile, crazed, obsessed. What if Aaron can't resist? What if it changes him, too, no matter how noble his intentions are now?

I latch onto the fear those thoughts summon and whirl around to face him. "And what is it, Aaron? Obsession? Bloodlust? I have enough of that in my life!"

Aaron frowns down at me without a flicker of the pain I expect. Instead, his brows are furrowed, reading between the lines. "What do you mean by bloodlust?"

Another stab of fear tears through me. I've said too much in my need to lash out. "Nothing," I snap before turning away, desperate for some distance.

In one quick stride, Aaron grasps my hand and spins me back toward him. When I crash into his chest, his hand cradles my neck, and he searches my eyes. "You panicked when I kissed your neck, and now you mention bloodlust. Luminita, does Vlad feed on you?" A snarl of disgust and anger accompanies the question, and it's enough to shake my resolve.

Tears constrict my throat again, and I can't speak, but I don't need to.

Rage builds until it boils over, flooding the room. "That soulless bastard!" he snarls between clenched teeth.

To my horror and dismay, fear takes control of my body, and I am powerless to stop it. "He is a strigoi. Of course, he has no soul." I shove away again, and he lets me. Those words cut him deep. Feeling that pain is hard enough without his touch amplifying it.

"I—" he starts, but the monster in control of me doesn't let him continue.

"Stop! You would do the same! It's not anger you feel. It's jealousy that heats your blood." It's not. I know that, but if he had a taste…if he knew the truth of me…it might be true.

Aaron's eyes widen with shock before the embers of his anger glow hot again. "You would compare *me* to *him*?" His teeth rake over his bottom lip, and he takes a step closer, but does not reach for me this time. "I worship you, offer you everything, while Vlad breaks your spirit more each year. He drinks from you like a damn prized cow and gods know what else! *I am *not* like *Vlad*!"

I swallow hard, wavering again, and he senses it.

One step brings him close, and his hands gently drift into my hair. The fractured thing in my chest rages, desperate for the reprieve he still offers.

"I cannot continue to witness him steal your fierceness, your divinity. You are but a ghost, and I want to bring you back to life, my beloved, my Goddess of blood and chaos."

The words sear into my very soul, ringing with truth. If anyone can bring me back to life, it is this man, and that scares me more than Vlad. Surrendering to it, giving in, and then losing it…would destroy me. It may only take one drop of my blood to change him, corrupt him. The risk is simply too great.

My palms shove at his chest, and he stumbles back, surprised. "I do *not* need your pity!" Every motion away from him cracks my heart a little deeper, but I pace to the window and focus on the gardens below.

"It is not pity," Aaron states softly.

"Then what is it?" I snap, without turning around.

I hear footsteps behind me, but he maintains some distance. "Thousands of years and I have never seen proof of a soul…until Orăştie, where we met. A vampire *can* have a soul. I know that with certainty. Whether you gifted it to me or simply brought it to life…I have one because of you, Luminita."

The fractures in my heart deepen to gaping fissures, and I try to keep my shoulders from shaking as tears roll down my cheeks. Even if I knew what to say, I couldn't get the words out.

He moves closer, and my body trembles. His hands slip around my waist, and I don't stop him. He gently tugs me back against him, and I don't pull away. His chin rests on my shoulder, and I want nothing more than to fall with him.

"Leave with me," he whispers against my hair.

"I can't." I hate saying the words.

The mere thought of returning to Suceava with Vlad, enduring more of his increasingly sadistic torments, shreds my insides. He knows I only have hate in my heart for him. That has only grown worse, and his frustration emerges violently when he forces me to his bed.

Vlad is only half strigoi, so I must be careful with the herbs, increase the doses slowly. At least the past handful of times he's violated me, the man has passed out before completion. Still…it's little comfort. They haven't had the desired effect yet. In fact, the Datura seeds seem to worsen his already vicious nature.

"We can run, Luminita. I will protect you."

"No," I say firmer this time. "You don't understand." I slip from his arms, though I'm reluctant to do so.

"What don't I understand?"

I glance over my shoulder before my gaze falls to the floor. "Vlad is…truly possessed. He will never let me go."

Dark violence gathers around him with the crackling energy of Ares himself. "Then I won't give him a choice."

The wrathful promise makes me turn on my heel. "You are but *one* man."

"I am *not* a *mere man*, and you know it."

Fear seizes my breath again because he's right, but that fact could be his downfall in many ways—exposure, imprisonment, my blood driving him mad, losing his life to save mine. *Prostul moare de grija alutia*—The fool dies worrying about someone else. That may be my fate, but it does not have to be his.

"Voivode Hunyadi intends to help him take the crown. Vlad will have *armies*."

"Which he will need to defend his crown, not hunt us," he counters.

Frustration blossoms beneath my skin, and I latch onto it, using it to put bite into my words. "He has made it *very* clear when he steals my blood and forces me to bed that he will sacrifice his crown and *everything* else standing between us to keep me. Betrayal will be met with further torment, and if anyone knows *you of all people* are here, it will only cause *me* more pain! You need to leave, not spout selfish things you mistake for romantic."

Aaron merely stares at me, lost in an ocean of conflicting emotions. The seconds stretch into what feels like an eternity while he works through my angry words. "He…violates you?" The question tumbles out of his mouth in disbelief, as if this thought had never occurred to him.

The sarcastic laugh that erupts from my throat is harsh. "What do you think a man *does* with his wife, Aaron? Or did you think I went to him willingly?"

"No," he states quickly, shaking his head. "I…didn't…I didn't want to think about it, I suppose."

"How convenient for you," I snap, wrapping my arms around myself again, trying to ignore the imprints of so many abuses.

"You cannot stay with him," he finally pleads in a heartbroken whisper.

I stuff everything in that dark pit to keep my resolve because I have no choice. Returning to Vlad is the only thing that keeps us both alive. "I can," I say defiantly, straightening my shoulders.

Aaron's brow furrows, his chest heaves, and he takes a step closer. "Lash out at me all you want, goddess, but now is not the time to prove a point. He's hurting you, and I *cannot* allow that!"

"You don't have a say in the matter. It is *my* choice, *my* decision, *not yours!*" I must move him from this path. Vlad will destroy him otherwise. I need to find a way to make Aaron stop before Vlad learns the full truth and torments us both for it.

Aaron's hand rakes through his hair, and a heavy sigh rushes past his lips. "Draga—"

"Stop calling me that!" Fear forces the scream from my mouth, and bone-deep regret seizes my insides. I can almost see the emotional wound it leaves behind. Fortunately for him, Aaron can't sense my feelings. Driving him away would be impossible if he could.

Still…he tries again. "Luminita—"

"Katharina," I correct sharply.

Tension fills his body, and I can sense his vulnerability retreating behind his gruff exterior. It simultaneously makes my heart heavy and eases my panic.

"Vlad can't lead an army if he's dead," he states in cold, simple terms.

"And how many men are you willing to slaughter? The Voivode? Do you plan to kill him?"

Aaron frowns, not following my logic.

"Because if you attack Vlad, *even* if you win, you will bring the wrath of Hunyadi, the boyar families, and *all* of Hungary down on us both!"

Frustration, rage, and disgust swirl through Aaron's signature as he starts to pace. "These are the rules of *humans!* They should have no bearing on us! They do not apply to us!"

"Has your ego made you so short-sighted? They *do* apply to us. They apply to the world, Aaron, and whether you like it or not, *you are not above it.* You need to leave before someone notices your presence here."

The strength leaks from him the longer he holds my frigid gaze, but he doesn't move.

"Leave now!" I point to the door, but avert my gaze. If I look at him now, wounded and emotionally bleeding, it will destroy my resolve.

Aaron stops before me, but I cannot meet his eyes. Tender fingers guide my chin, tilting my face toward his. When my eyes meet his, I hide behind all my masks and excuses, using them as armor to keep me from falling apart. Somehow, I manage to glare into his tear-filled eyes.

"I will figure out a way to save you. I swear it."

Something in me breaks…shatters…and a cold, venomous voice speaks through my mouth, taking over again, leaving me powerless to do anything other than watch in horror. "I don't *need you* to save me."

The sharp words strike true, and he swallows hard. "You *need* no one. You've made that more than clear."

Inside the words make me weep, but I have no control over my body. "Obviously not clear enough."

I can actually *feel* the crack those words cause in his heart, and I need it to stop. I need this hell to stop. I fight and rage against my fear, desperate to take it all back, to tell him the truth…all of it. But it's like banging my fists against a stone wall.

"I'll help you regardless," the words emerge on a heartbreaking sigh.

"Why?" My fear snarls the question like a rabid wolf.

Aaron searches my eyes as if he knows this is not me…that I'm lost inside somewhere. Tears slip down his cheeks. "Because *I* am the one who needs *you*."

I try desperately to reach the surface of my own mind, to wrestle control from the cold, unfeeling thing speaking, but I am drowning in my tears, unable to find my way back to him.

"I don't care."

Aaron shakes his head, pressing his forehead to mine. "I *know* that's not true."

"Then I will hate you until it's true." Those words…the same ones he spoke to me after Dragobete, hit like a death blow to us both, though Aaron can't see my torment through the monster's mask.

He recoils, backing up a step. "Why would you—"

"Is that not what you told me?" My fear keeps pressing, slashing at him with words that can never be unsaid. My body moves forward, and he backs up another step, heart racing. "Now you wish to be a hero? After casting me aside? After swearing your undying hatred?"

Aaron stiffens and doesn't move when the monster prowls forward. "No. You are trying to drive me away. You know none of that is true."

He is right, but my fear refuses to give up control. It holds his gaze with a glare full of fury I don't feel. "Get out!"

Aaron grips my arms. "This is *not* you. I know better."

Of course, he does. The man loves me, and as much as I try to deny it, I love him too.

"You know *nothing*!" my fear growls with a venomous bite. "Get your hands off me and leave!"

Aaron's throat bobs, and fresh tears fill his eyes. His hands slowly fall from my arms, and his shoulders slump forward. "As you wish, my goddess."

The raw agony in his words almost gives me the strength to take back control, but it isn't until he leaves and closes the door behind him that the cold monster retreats, abandoning me to the aftermath.

I sink to my knees, wrap my arms around my stomach, and weep in heaving sobs for every wound I've caused us both.

16.   Belgrade

Aaron

I move swiftly down the hall with my wounded heart thrashing mindlessly against my ribs. I have to put distance between us. If I don't, I'll run right back to her, and I'm not certain how much more poison I can take today. She doesn't mean those things. I know she doesn't, but they sliced me to ribbons regardless.

I am also aware that I cannot be in the same room with Vlad. The second I lay eyes on him, I won't be able to stop. I'll end up ripping off his perverse manhood and ramming it down his throat for what he's done.

I try not to think about it, but the sins consume my thoughts anyway. Forcibly drinking from her is a grave enough offense without his hands…his mouth…his lecherous cock violating her, taking her against her will. It all sours and twists my stomach painfully.

Human laws don't care. She is his wife. Everything he's done is within his rights in their eyes and those of their infernal god, but *not* mine. Vlad Dracul has committed atrocities against the *only* goddess I worship, and he *will* know my wrath…eventually. As much as it angers me, Luminita is right. *Today* is *not* that day.

I round the corner into the main hall, and one voice stops me dead in my tracks. "General Bogdan."

My chest heaves as I slowly look over my shoulder, my eyes narrowing to deadly points.

Vlad Dracul storms toward me, his hands balled into fists at his side. I can already see he's made the connection. After all, I just walked out of the hall where his room is…one I have no business being down. To hell with best laid plans. Let it be today after all.

The world is nothing but an ocean of red as I whirl around, meet him in the center of the hall, and slug him so hard in the jaw his head jerks violently sideways. He stumbles, stunned, and I have my knife out before I can even comprehend the severity of my situation. I haul him up by his dragon-embroidered collar and shove him hard against the stone pillar.

I stare into Vlad's furious eyes, my blade at his throat. "You will pay for what you've done," I growl each word slowly, so he retains them. It isn't a threat. It is a promise.

"Bogdan!" I hear John shout my name from a distance.

Vlad's lips tip up into a grin. This is precisely what he wanted.

My gaze cuts to John, who is storming down the hall, but he's still quite a way off. Unfortunately, Vlad takes advantage of my momentary distraction.

The man moves quickly, snatching my wrist and slamming the blade's hilt into my face. It doesn't hurt much, but he uses the momentary shock to shove me off, spin me around, and slam my back into the pillar. Suddenly, my blade is at *my* throat.

Vlad's eyes darken as he leans in close. "I could slice your throat right here, right now, and suffer no repercussions." A wicked grin curls his lips beneath his thick moustache. "Do you know why I won't?"

I swallow hard, my neck pressing into the blade with the motion, but not enough to break the skin.

"Because you give her hope."

The words make my stomach sink.

"As long as you're alive, I can continue to break her…bit…by…bit."

The rage that consumes me is absolute, but with the blade pressed tight to my throat, there is little I can do. I may be a vampire, but I still bleed.

"Have you ever tasted her?" His head tilts as if honestly curious about my answer. His eyes rake over my face, and that grin widens. "No. I don't suppose you have. If you'd tasted her, you would fight harder than a lovesick dog. It's pure magic." A sickening sigh of pleasure escapes the man, and my bile rises.

I hear John's hurried footsteps coming closer.

Vlad leans forward, whispering into my ear. "Just so you know, tonight I will erase any trace you've left on her. As is my right as her husband."

"Vlad! Bogdan!" John's firm voice bellows, echoing off the walls.

Vlad steps back enough to flash his malicious grin and then shoves away from me. He tosses the knife at my feet, knowing I can't attack him in front of the Voivode without risking not just my life, but Luminita's. If I try to kill him and fail, she will suffer far worse than what he's threatened.

"What in the name of all that is holy is going on?" John shouts as he storms up to us.

Vlad pulls on a polite smile and adjusts his doublet. "A disagreement between gentlemen, nothing more. Isn't that right, Bogdan?" His gaze shifts to me with a devilish glint.

Every fiber in my body wants to rend him apart and take my time doing a slow and thorough job. "Yes." I force the vile word past my lips.

I can feel John's gaze on me, but mine stays fixed on the hateful demon before me.

"Bogdan, take a walk. Vlad, come with me." John's firm command leaves no room for argument.

After Vlad flashes me another sly grin and mouths the words "my wife", he turns to John. "Of course, Voivode. I am happy to comply."

Only when he walks toward the Voivode does my gaze move to John. He's angry, of course, but there is a sadness there as well.

"Take a walk," he repeats.

I push away from the pillar and march toward the front doors. The blood pounds so violently in my ears that I can't hear anything else. I have to force each and every step away from Vlad. I can't even try to kill him in secret now. I've publicly made my hatred for the man more than clear.

As I near the front doors, I spot my little errand boy from earlier and whistle sharply. He hurries over with a bright smile despite the hateful scowl fixed on my face. He's probably eager for another florin.

The boy runs to match my hurried pace. "Yes, Sir?"

"I need you to deliver a message to the Voivode."

He frowns at me, confused, peeking over his shoulder.

"In a few minutes' time," I clarify. "Tell him I've had urgent news and need to leave. I'm not certain when I'll return."

The boy nods.

I dig into my pocket and toss him another gold coin.

He sprints off in the opposite direction.

My hurried footsteps halt at the front door, and I peer back at the entrance to the East Hall, where Luminita is. I can still feel the pull...the thing drawing me toward her, but I can't help her right now. She's made her choice, and my impetuous anger has cost me any leverage I might have had. Besides, I can't take any more pain tonight.

She's pushing me away on purpose. She does not mean those things. She *can't* mean them and respond to me the way she does. However, even false words cut deep, and on top of Vlad's comments, I am more of a danger to her here. I need to slink away, lick my wounds, and come up with a plan.

I force my stare away from her direction and march toward the stables. I have no food, no water, no provisions, but I can acquire those in the next town. I need to be away from this place…as far away from Lord and Lady Dracul as I can be.

My hands move by memory, saddling and bridling my horse, whom I named Kali in secret honor of my own goddess of blood and chaos. The thought of abandoning her to that monster turns my stomach until my hands still and the bile rises once more. There is power in numbers, and by morning, Vlad will have a measure of control over several armies, including mine.

I climb into the saddle and head southwest, toward Belgrade. That's where the rumors of Sultan Mehmed the Second's plans for war originated. Perhaps I'll be lucky and find a band of Turks to unleash my violent rage upon. The *need* to make something suffer is all-consuming.

It's then that I realize I haven't fed today. I'll have to find more than provisions in the next town. Blood and chaos are what I require, which only reminds me of my goddess. I urge my horse into a gallop, riding hard. I nearly lose my will and return to her regardless of the consequences.

17.   How Villains are Made

Luminita
Suceava Court – October 1455

The needle jabs my willowy finger, and I barely flinch before continuing to work the embroidery thread through the fabric. I watch the blood spread, soaking the white strands bit by bit. My blood is a curse that has snared me, trapped me in a prison of perpetual torment, which has only grown worse over the past two years.

"Good morning, Katharina, my love." Vlad's voice elicits no reaction from me. Anger growls over my skin, but still, I give him nothing. My fingers weave the thread through the fabric despondently.

Vlad forced blood from me last night, and I will no longer grant him my reactions. Maybe then he'll grow bored.

"Your tea is getting cold," I nod toward the poisoned brew. I added more Datura today, but I'm growing impatient. Dark circles ring his eyes, and he's a bit weak, but not noticeably so.

It's beyond humiliating, submitting to a weak, depraved man, but his threats still hold weight. I didn't break Aaron's heart just to condemn him now. Failure to comply means Aaron suffers the price, and I have hurt him enough.

"I have no stomach for it today," Vlad grumbles. "Besides, the servants will be here shortly to help us pack."

The needle pauses, and I peer over at the man.

"I received word today from Voivode Hunyadi. He has granted us asylum at his court and is requesting my presence immediately."

"We are moving to Beszterce?" I keep a stranglehold on my emotions, giving him nothing.

"Yes, wife. I will ride ahead. You may travel with the cart and belongings when they are ready."

I nod and pull the thread through the bloodstain.

Vlad grips my chin and angles my face toward him to search my eyes. "You still belong to me, my love."

Slowly, my eyes rise to meet his with a distant stare. "A point you have made clear many times." I do not even give the man the satisfaction of my anger.

His blue-grey eyes narrow. "You will forgive me one day and recall how to love me."

A smile unfurls across my lips, but I give him nothing else. "There are not enough days in existence for that to be the case."

Those frigid eyes narrow. "Do you know much of Dacian customs?"

The odd and unexpected question captures my attention, but I lower my gaze to the needle in my hand. "Yes."

Vlad settles into the chair in front of me. His stare is full of threats, and my heart races a little faster. The man is smart in his cruelty, and I have no idea where his mind is going. All I know is that it's never a good place.

"You're aware then of how important mothers are in our culture?"

My eyes lift from the fabric in my hands while cold clenches my insides. I hadn't known he was Dacian, and this particular subject seems dangerous.

"Yes," I respond tentatively.

His expression doesn't change. "They care intently for their children without the influence of men for the first ten years of life."

Again, his words surprise me. I had thought he meant to address the fact that I have yet to give him an heir, despite his constant…attention. "I am aware."

Vlad's gaze narrows in the assessing manner I frequently see before he peers toward the window. "My mother was a failure. She left me and Mircea…took her own life when I was seven. She didn't have the strength to care for us." The disdain in his voice terrifies me.

"It's because of her *selfish act* we were forced to leave Schassburg…our peaceful home." Vlad's lip curls, and a muscle twitches in his jaw before he continues.

Draga & the Savage: Dracul

"My father moved us to Târgovişte. Unless you were among the established boyar families, it was a rundown city full of corruption and crime, and I was thrust into the world of violent men too early."

Anger burns in the pit, but I keep it from Vlad. The gall of this man…justifying his crimes with *this*…turns my stomach.

His gaze slides back to me, and for a moment, I wonder if my control has slipped…if he senses my anger. Perhaps he is merely waiting for a reaction. Vlad's eyes rake over me coldly, but he continues to speak.

"My one mercy was my elder brother Mircea. I worshipped him. We were educated by the same tutors, practiced swordplay, all the things young men require."

When his gaze drifts to the floor, a well of sadness, pain, and rage consumes him like an inferno. "When Sultan Murad demanded a sacrifice from my father, he did not ask for me and Radu. Did you know that?"

Vlad locks eyes with me then.

"No," I answer honestly.

His head tilts, blue-grey eyes narrowing again. "Why have you never asked about my past?"

I boldly stare back and speak the truth. "Because I do not care."

The muscle in his jaw ticks again, and the skin around his eyes tightens. "You should, wife. After all, you experience the result of it."

The ominous message creeps through the air like the fingers of death itself, and I fight to control my pulse.

"Sultan Murad specifically asked for Mircea as a show of faith from my father. But Mircea was the only one of us he cared for. He saw me as weak, and Radu, my younger brother, was from his loveless second marriage. So, he sent us in Mircea's place."

Vlad leans forward and rests his forearms on his knees. "Have you ever been to Kutahya Egrigoz Castle?"

I shake my head, unable to speak when violence fills his entire being.

"I'm certain even your *Savage* would find it barbaric. They made butchery and sodomy their profession, one Radu and I were not immune to."

Vlad's stare drifts away from me then, and raw pain emanates from him like an overwhelming flood. "Soldiers brought piles of tongues, severed heads, and dismembered male genitalia as offerings. I was locked away in a small cell and beaten for days if I dared voice a word they disliked, and there were many. Sometimes they simply beat and burned us for fun."

He swallows hard, and I swear, his eyes glisten with tears. "They forced themselves on me in public view, an act that was not only condoned, but encouraged."

And yet he forces himself on me, beats me, burns me, despite *knowing* the pain it causes. It only makes me hate him more.

"When I became a man, they moved me to Tokat, taught me their language, battle skills, horsemanship…" The malicious glare returns to me. "They forced me to torture others, to inflict the same pain I was dealt, to watch them impale their prisoners on stakes."

My blood feels like ice in my veins, and drawing in a breath takes an effort.

Vlad leans forward more, one corner of his cruel mouth tilting up while horrific malevolence burns in his eyes. "*All of it*…everything I have endured…happened because of the *weakness* and *selfishness* of a woman."

Suddenly, everything makes sense, and I struggle to swallow the fear threatening to drown me. Had I known his past, perhaps I could have pieced things together sooner, avoided him, saved myself from this eternal torment.

The same assessing glare rakes over my body with so much venom, I feel it poisoning my blood…my very soul. He rises and stalks closer, bending to whisper. "You are selfish, my love, but…you are not weak. At least, your blood is not. But I'll tell you a secret, my dearest wife. Something I learned in Turkey."

His hand snatches my hair tight, and I grimace. "One day, you'll miss my touch, crave it…you'll *need* the pain. You'll seek it out, force it from others. This is how villains are made, my love."

The words sink into my marrow with a deathly chill I cannot hide.

Vlad purrs against my ear. "There it is, my delicious wife. The fear only truth can bring." He presses a kiss to my temple, his lips lingering against my skin. "I crave you too, you know. Not just your blood. Your wicked tongue is capable of quite delightful things when properly motivated."

Despite my resolve, my stomach sours and twists.

Vlad laughs. "Even your disgust is a sweet torment I would miss in your absence."

My heart races while I struggle to regain control of my emotions. Vlad bends, his mouth hovering beside my ear. "Can you still feel me, my wife?" His teeth graze my earlobe, and I jerk away from him, but I don't wear the sneer he desires.

Draga & the Savage: Dracul

My entire body is a patchwork of imprints, predominantly Vlad's sadistic glee. It pulses over my skin in a perpetual state, tormenting me long after he's appeased himself. Vlad does not know the truth of that ability, however. That is a secret I have been able to keep from him.

There is one spot…just below my navel where Aaron's loving touch still clings to my skin. My hand often drifts there in search of reprieve.

Vlad's dark laugh pulls me from my thoughts. "Bogdan is still in Belgrade, if you're curious."

I straighten and stuff everything into that pit. "I am not," I state in clipped tones.

"Such pretty lies."

I can see his creeping grin from the corner of my eye.

"Keep in mind, my love, Bogdan is not at Beszterce to defend himself. I can tell the Voivode whatever I want. I could even tell him the General attacked you. You can deny it, of course, but the word of a woman counts for nothing. Do *not* delay your arrival or consider running. I'll find you *after* I ensure Bogdan suffers to my satisfaction."

My gaze falls back to the fabric in my hands. I shove the needle through and pull, but the threat rattles me, and Vlad is aware of it.

Travelling with a cart and servants will take twice the time…ten days at least. For three days now, my fractured and beaten heart races with Vlad's threat repeating in my mind. Not even conducting my sage ritual in secret helps quell the panic and melancholy. It doesn't make the imprints fade either. They still torment me continually.

I should kill him. Take his despicable life, whether or not it ends mine. The thought hardens inside me as the days drag on. Survival is not worth this perpetual cost. Vlad could live for a hundred years or more, and the idea of enduring like *this* for that long…horrifies me more than death.

As if the weather senses my growing gloom, the dark skies rip open on the fifth day of our journey. Cold soaks into my bones either due to the Autumn rain or the receding distance between me and my tormentor. When my skin goes numb and the chill inside persists, I know it is the latter. I cannot even enjoy these days apart because Vlad is already in Beszterce…capable of dooming both me and Aaron. My fate rests on the vicious whims of a *man*. The very thing I fought so hard to avoid my entire life.

I cannot even blame my father for marrying me away or my brother for bringing war upon our house. I entered into this willingly. I foolishly believed I could control the strigoi. Of course, I did not know the effect my blood would have on him.

It makes me wonder if that is why Aaron desires me with such fervor. Does my blood call to him? Does it seduce him, even if he does not realize it?

I pull the wet blanket tighter around me, but it does nothing to warm me.

18.   Sibiu

Aaron
Beszterce Court

The long, hard ride from Belgrade has left me exhausted, but the news must be delivered in person. I stop my horse outside the stable and toss the reins to the young man who runs out to greet me.

"Take good care of her. She's had a rough ten days." I pat the majestic beast's flank, and Kali neighs, nodding as if she agrees.

The man merely stares at me like I've spoken a foreign language. He isn't new. He's worked with the horses for at least the past six years. Some days, I think Kali is more intelligent than the humans who care for her.

I jog toward the palace, passing several vaguely familiar courtiers and the front guards without much notice.

"General Bogdan, Sir!" an almost familiar voice shouts. He sounds older than I recall. The young lad who helped me before I left for Belgrade has shot up at least a head's length.

"Is Voivode Hunyadi in his chambers?"

The boy nods with an expectant smile.

"A florin? For simple information?" My eyebrow arches, but I wear a slight grin.

The boy shrugs and holds out his palm. There was a time when I used to scare small children. Now they extort coin from me with ease, it seems. I've spent too much time among humans.

After tossing the grinning fool a coin, I continue to John's chambers. I only knock briefly before I barge inside, and the world screeches to a halt.

I have precious seconds to school my expression and snuff out the soul-searing rage Vlad Dracul summons. It's rather challenging with his taunts and threats still echoing in my head as vividly as the day they slithered from his venomous mouth.

"By God's bones, Bogdan! Are you trying to stop a man's heart?" John clutches his chest and drags in several deep breaths.

"My apologies. I only just arrived." I keep my eyes fixed on John, trying to ignore the monster in our midst. "I have urgent news."

"Well, come in, come in." John waves an impatient hand, and I force my feet forward, avoiding Vlad's cutting stare.

John seems unbothered by having us in the same room, so it seems Vlad decided to stick with the cover of our *disagreement between gentlemen*. If I make a point of kicking him out now, it will only weaken my position.

"I have confirmed with certainty Sultan Mehmed the Second's intention to attack Belgrade. Zagan, Mahmud, and Karaca are leading one hundred thousand men or more. They have cannons and siege engines, John."

The Voivode's face turns to a mask of cold calculation, his mind working the problem. "How long do we have?"

"June…maybe July if we can slow them down."

John nods thoughtfully. "I'll send for Mihaly and Laszlo. We'll send letters to the papal legate, John of Capistrano, and Durad Brankovic—"

"Brankovic?" I ask, honestly surprised. "The man who ransomed you and nearly handed you over to the same Turks we intend to fight?"

"Times change. He has quite the vendetta against the Turks now. It will outweigh our petty rivalry from years ago. His mercenaries are well-trained, and there's every possibility he will lead a charge before the Turks reach Belgrade if we act fast enough."

"Why the friar?" Vlad speaks up for the first time since my arrival, and merely the sound of his gruff voice stirs my blood.

"He has a way with the people. If Bogdan is correct about the Ottoman Empire's numbers, we will need a peasant army to supplement our own, even with Brankovic's help." John stands to pace, rubbing his chin while forming a plan. "I have five thousand mercenaries I can send to Belgrade now with my brother-in-law and Laszlo. I can raise another two thousand in and around Beszterce."

The Voivode comes to a stop in front of Vlad, assessing him for a few moments. His gaze flicks to me for an instant, and then he stares hard at Vlad. "You'll take a small army of Romanian soldiers to guard Sibiu and the Transylvanian passes."

Draga & the Savage: Dracul

Vlad bristles while I clench my jaw to keep from smiling. "But Sibiu is not their target."

John's thick eyebrows lift almost to his receding hairline, and my smile almost breaks free. "Are you too good to guard the critical gateway between Wallachia and the rest of our empire?"

"No, Sir. It's just that I feel my skills would be better suited—"

"Do you?" John interrupts furiously. "So, it's *my judgment* you find in question? How many wars have you plotted a defense for, Vlad Dracul? How many battles have you fought and *won*?"

I keep my eyes forward and let Vlad dig his own grave while still fighting the grin that longs to break free.

"None, Sir," Vlad says in a quieter voice, bowing his head. "I apologize for questioning your orders."

"As you damn well should. You'll gather the men now and head out in four days' time for Sibiu."

"But Sir, my wife—"

"Is *not* a subject I wish to discuss in *my war room*! *Four days* or you lose my support."

Vlad bows his head again, and I must admit, this is the best day I've had since I left Beszterce.

"You are dismissed to make your arrangements, Lord Dracul."

My eyes remain firmly fixed ahead, but…I do allow myself a grin.

Vlad's glare holds an excessive amount of poison, which naturally makes my grin spread wider. I desperately want to tell Vlad that I'll be more than happy to see to his wife, but John would not appreciate me crossing that line. Especially, in light of what John just did.

I'd still do it, but I have the upper hand for the moment, and I'd like to keep it.

Vlad storms out of the room, and the door slams behind him. Only then does the tension leave my shoulders.

"Sibiu?" I ask, unable to hold back my laugh.

John shrugs as he continues to glare at the door. "The boy is glory-hungry to a fault. He needs to learn patience. A few months guarding the Turnu Rosu Pass should do it."

John's stare finally slides to me. "And *where* have you been?"

"I thought that would be obvious. Belgrade."

The man's cunning eyes narrow on me, and his arms fold over his chest. "Let me see if I understand the order of events here. Lord and Lady Dracul arrive at court. The Lady retires to her quarters, and I take

Vlad to speak in private. You are due to join us, but *instead*, I find you two brawling in the main hall. *After that*, you send some cryptic message about leaving with no idea when you'd return. *Then* I don't hear from you for *six god forsaken months!*"

"I wrote to you when I had news. It took the better part of a month just to get there, John."

"And the Lady Dracul has *nothing* to do with this *urgent news*, I suppose?"

"Of course, not," I state with well-practiced simplicity. It isn't a complete lie. She may have been a contributing factor to my departure, but I had no idea they were at court when I arrived.

John releases an exasperated sigh. "You are absolutely infuriating. After so many years by my side, do you *truly* think me a fool?"

I meet his eyes then with a somber expression. "No, my friend. I do not."

"Yet you lie to me?"

All these irritating rules of men. Why do I feel I owe him an explanation?

"You are the Voivode of Wallachia, Regent for the Kingdom of Hungary first and foremost."

John's gaze shifts once again, working the problem. "Then don't force my hand. You are my friend, my companion in war. I know you pity the poor creature. I even understand why, especially lately."

The last words make my blood run cold. "What do you mean?"

John frowns up at me with one raised eyebrow. "You seem awfully concerned."

I close my eyes for a moment and draw in a deep breath. "Fine. I *am* concerned for her welfare."

"She seemed unwell…frail even, the last few times at court, even more so than the day you left. She isn't meant to arrive until after I ordered Vlad to leave." John chews the inside of his cheek.

"It seems you are concerned for her safety as well," I say.

John peers up at me. "I *am* concerned for her, but more so for *you*."

Confusion wrinkles my brow. "If you kill Vlad, a damned royal heir to the Romanian throne of Wallachia, I'll have no choice but to order your execution. That is not something I wish to sign my name to. Had you been here when they were last at court, I'm certain you would have forced me to."

Dread clutches my heart and squeezes until the agony is almost unbearable. "When is she due to arrive?"

John sighs and eyes me cautiously. "Bogdan."

"When?" I demand in a firmer voice.

"Five days, maybe six. They are moving here to court. I granted them asylum. She's travelling with her servants and possessions."

I turn to the door, but John claps a hand on my shoulder and spins me back. "What are you doing?"

"I'll ride out…ensure she arrives safely."

"You can't touch him, Bogdan."

"I know." The growled words vibrate in my aching chest.

Another heavy huff of air leaves the man. "When you find them, send the servants ahead. Tell them I'm sending Vlad to Sibiu, and he requires his things *before* he leaves. Ensure you do *nothing* untoward until they're gone. If one witness comes to me, I will have no choice but to defend Vlad's *honor*." A sneer accompanies the last word. "Take your time getting back. Ensure Vlad leaves *before* you arrive. That's all I can do for you, my friend."

For the first time in a very long time, I feel genuine gratitude toward a human. "Thank you, John."

"Please, don't make me sign your death warrant. I'm not a young man, and you're my last remaining friend."

A snorting laugh escapes me despite everything. "John. This may surprise you, but you're the only friend I've ever had."

John bellows a hearty laugh. "*That*, I do believe. Be safe, be careful, and take my horse. Kali needs to rest."

I nod before racing into the hall in search of the extorting errand boy. I find him in the main hall, peeking into the court. It occurs to me I don't know the child's name, so I whistle.

He scurries over with that same expectant smile. "What's your name?"

"Andrei, Sir."

I force a smile. Polite small talk is not my area of expertise, especially with the smaller humans. "Andrei, I need you to go to the kitchens. Get me at least a week's rations."

"Are you heading back out so soon, Sir?"

"Yes, on an urgent matter. Meet me in the Voivode's stable." I slip two florins into his palm, and his little eyes light up. "As fast as you can."

19.   Sadness

Luminita

Although the rain has stopped, a thick mist still surrounds us with chilling cold. The morning sun peeks above the trees, but it is not enough to warm me. Perhaps nothing ever will. Every move closer to Beszterce twists my guts a bit more, and my blood feels like icy sludge in my veins.

I stare despondently down at my thin hands as the cart sways. They look so frail…skin stretched over bone. They held such power once, controlled my fate. Hopefully, they have one last desperate act of strength within them. When I arrive at Beszterce, I will drain Vlad and resign myself to execution. It will be the final time I control my future…one last act of independence.

Pounding hooves approach from the direction of Beszterce, and my heart sinks faster. I keep my gaze down, locked on my pale palms. Vlad must have grown impatient. How annoyingly typical. Even now, he disrupts my plans.

The wagon and horses come to a jolting halt, but I don't lift my eyes, don't use my senses, don't give the vicious monster any of my consideration. I am a fortress with impassive mental walls I intend to hold firmly in place.

Boots hit the ground, and servants begin to speak in hushed voices. The footsteps approach me, squishing in the mud, and despite my resolve, my hands shake, and tears fill my eyes. I was supposed to have three more days…three more days to prepare for the end of my over five hundred years of life. Of course, Vlad would rob me of that, too.

I feel his body heat at my side, hear his heavy breathing, but something strange tingles across my mental armor like a gut-wrenchingly sad caress. Vlad is *never* gentle in *anything* he does, not anymore.

My tired eyes finally lift, and the relief that floods my body rips tears from my eyes.

"Katharina," Aaron says in a quiet tone meant just for me. "Just do as I say...*please*."

Even if I had the strength to deny his plea, I don't want to. I nod once, and the heartbreak in his eyes fills me with shame. I must disgust him...weak and frail as I am now. After averting my eyes with my mental walls still in place, I pull the wet blanket tighter around my shoulders.

Aaron takes a few steps back and raises his voice. "Lord Dracul is being sent to Sibiu on orders from the Voivode. He leaves in two days' time and requires his things."

Despair grips my heart in its clutches, squeezing painfully. No doubt I am counted among *his things*.

"The Voivode requested I escort the Lady Dracul at a slower pace, since she is unwell and will *not* be traveling to Sibiu."

My eyes snap up to Aaron's in surprise, and a slight smile lifts the corner of his mouth.

The servants' whispers grow to murmurs of discontent, and Aaron's attention moves to them with a scowl.

"Silence!" he commands. "You are all to continue to Beszterce in double-time. The Voivode Hunyadi demands it!"

Everyone scurries into motion, and Aaron approaches me once more. He maintains a respectful distance and holds out his hand. His throat bobs, and I lower my shields enough to sense his nervousness, sadness, barely-restrained need, even the seething hatred...which I hope is not for me. I don't think I could survive his anger right now, even though I deserve it.

I slip my shaky hand into his. It looks so pale against his tanned skin. After collecting my remaining strength, I rise, and he guides me to the edge of the cart.

"May I help you down, Lady Dracul?" he asks, loud enough for the servants to hear, but an undercurrent of rage accompanies the surname.

"Please." I try to speak loud and clear, but I haven't used my voice in days. The words emerge trembling and rough.

Aaron's brow falls, and his eyes mist. Sadness...it's all I sense from him. Not pity or disgust, just sadness...overwhelming, all-consuming sadness.

His hands gently grip my small waist, and the sensation worsens, which I hadn't even thought possible. I have not had much of an appetite in quite some time. Once he lifts me out of the cart and sets me on my feet, frustration overtakes his sadness.

Aaron's hands leave me, and my knees buckle. I've been sitting for days, and I'm weak. Not only have I not been eating much food, but I also haven't drawn energy from others either. I want *nothing* from Vlad unless it is to take his life, and he often locks me away…prevents me from using my gifts. It's left me too scared to pull from another. I would lose control, drain them completely, and be labeled a witch or a murderer.

I don't hit the mud, however. Aaron catches me and sweeps me into his arms. For a moment, he stares at me, but his attention turns back to the servants.

"The Lady Dracul is sicker than expected. We will ride to the next town and seek a healer. Please inform the Voivode."

"What about Lord Dracul? Should he not know?" One of the male servants stands out among the rest. The others merely frown at him in disapproval.

"Inform the Voivode!" Aaron repeats firmly. "*He* can inform Lord Dracul, if he wishes to do so."

Aaron strides toward his horse, and as much as I wish to simply collapse against his chest and weep, I don't. That would be unbecoming for a married woman, sick or not. Aaron is desperately trying to keep things proper in front of the servants. The least I can do is not ruin his efforts.

He moves around the warhorse, putting the massive beast between us and the scrambling servants. Then the tears come for us both. Aaron presses his forehead to mine, and it's all I can do to keep from openly sobbing.

"I am so sorry." His voice cracks, and so does my already beaten and battered heart.

I say nothing because I can't. My throat constricts around a thousand things I wish to say. None of them manages to escape.

Horses begin to move, the wagon creaks, and Aaron sets me on my feet with the horse against my back to steady me. He takes a step back with considerable effort, forcing the socially acceptable distance, and turns his gaze toward the servants as they begin to pass.

I take in the rapid rise and fall of his broad chest, the stern set of his jaw, the streaks of grey in his dark hair, which seem more pronounced, the morning sun on his warm skin, and the lines that bracket his mouth on the rare occasions he smiles.

Vlad leaves in two days, and Aaron intends to take me to a healer. I won't have to see Vlad. He will be gone before I arrive. I have no idea for how long, but I have some measure of freedom from Vlad's cruelty.

The patchwork of imprints flickers along my skin, reminding me of their wretched existence. It will take a *long* time for them to fade…for me to be truly free…if it is even possible.

Vlad's words still haunt me. *One day, you'll miss my touch, crave it…you'll need the pain. You'll seek it out, force it from others. This is how villains are made, my love.*

Is that my future? Perhaps. But if I survive this, I will find a way to ensure it *never* happens again. I will scour the earth and find some way to increase my power…to rise above the laws of mortal men…to be beyond reproach…to carve *my own* path…always. No matter the cost.

The last servant passes from view, and Aaron is before me in an instant. His warm arms fold around me, pulling me against his heaving chest. I collapse against him and sob for every injustice Vlad has dealt, for becoming this wrecked creature, for *allowing* this to happen.

Aaron's arms tighten, and he places a kiss in my hair with a tear-filled sigh. "I never should have left for Belgrade."

With some effort, the tears slow enough for me to speak, though barely. "You could not have done anything. It just would have been worse for us both."

His hard swallow echoes in my ear, and he pulls back enough to meet my eyes. "I *am* taking you to a healer. When was the last time you ate?"

I stare at his chest, ashamed. I don't know the answer. Days?

Aaron drags in a shaky breath. "I will find a way to make him pay, Luminita Dragomir. *We* will *both* make him pay. Do you hear me?"

When I don't respond, he lifts my chin with a tender touch. I'm sure he sees the doubt and defeat in my tired eyes.

"Can you keep your balance on the horse? Long enough for me to mount?"

I nod slowly.

Once again, he wraps his hands around my waist. He lifts me up to the saddle and holds onto me until I grip the pommel. I manage to keep myself upright while he climbs up behind me, but it takes more effort than I thought.

Aaron pulls me to his chest, and I curl up against him. I listen to the steady beat of his heart while we ride at a gentle pace through the forest.

This comfort won't last. I know that. The risk from my blood is too great. Knowing Vlad's past as I do now…there's a chance my blood didn't make him crazed, that he was already that way. But…if that is not the case, I cannot risk losing Aaron to madness. One taste could change him forever.

Right now, however…I need him. I can't push him away, not even for his own safety. I can't lash out to protect him from me. I won't make it through this without him.

Vlad was wrong. I am both selfish *and* weak.

20.　Poiana Negrii

Aaron

We ride southwest, heading for Poiana Negrii, a small village I've visited *many* times. The citizens there have proven their discretion over the years.

Luminita shivers against me, and I wrap an arm tight around her, wishing I could undo everything she's endured. The vibrant Goddess of blood and chaos that brought me to my knees is little more than skin and bones. Even her once luminous eyes are dull and sunken, surrounded by dark circles.

I rest my cheek upon her head and struggle to contain all these emotions. They are so unfamiliar to me. There was a time, I had one…maybe two of them. More often than not, I've been apathetic at best during my long existence. It made sense back then…not believing in a soul.

However, since our paths crossed, I cannot deny owning one any longer. It's painful, especially now, but those moments of euphoria, no matter how brief…they are worth *any* pain.

Luminita's sharp words from our last encounter return to me in vivid color. They still tear at me, but I would endure them all again and worse for her. I know that with certainty. I *knew* that back on Dragobete. She is the addiction from which I will never recover.

"I know people in Poiana Negrii," I say, hoping she isn't asleep. She's tired…exhausted, but I need to hear her voice, no matter how frail it is. "They will give us a place to stay with a warm fire, hot food, and I will bring you a healer."

Jenny Allen

She says nothing at first, but then she shifts slightly. "Are you teasing me with warm thoughts, Sălbatic?" Her voice is faint, but the humor and use of my nickname give me hope.

A small chuckle rumbles in my chest. "Merely giving you something to look forward to." I press a kiss into her hair and squeeze her against me a little tighter.

"You've already done that. A few days…of freedom."

"More than a few days. Hunyadi is sending him to Sibiu to guard the pass until July, most likely. There is a war coming."

"Then perhaps there is a god, and he will claim Vlad's wretched soul for me."

My jaw clenches painfully tight on a hard swallow before I growl the words. "He deserves worse."

"Far worse," she whispers in a haunted tone. "But…"

"But what?" Dread creeps into my chest, and I know she feels it.

"Nothing," she says with a sigh.

"Luminita, if you draw on me…take some of my essence, will it help you?"

"I simply need food and a warm bed to rest," she states, avoiding the question.

"Will it help you?" I repeat a little firmer.

She says nothing.

"Take what you need from me."

"No," she says softly.

"Why not?" Whether or not it's intended, the refusal feels like rejection.

She doesn't respond at first but releases a weary breath. "When you go too long without drinking blood, what happens when you do?"

"I am less discreet with my choices, reckless…" The answer in her question clicks then. "And yes, control is difficult."

"I do not wish to hurt you more than I already have." The whispered confession weighs heavily on my heart.

We're quiet for a time, and when I peer down, I find her asleep against my chest. Thick lashes rest against the smudges of purple beneath her eyes, but she looks…peaceful. It's little comfort, but better than nothing.

Draga & the Savage: Dracul

Dumitru, the village elder, runs to meet us within minutes of our arrival in Poiana Negrii. "Lord Aaron!" He breathes heavily from the brief sprint. "We were not expecting you. It's been some time."

"Travel that couldn't be helped." I carefully dig into my pocket, not wanting to jostle Luminita. She's still sleeping, despite Dumitru's shout. I pass him a handful of gold florins, and the man's eyes widen.

"I require lodgings for a few days, as well as our usual arrangement."

"That can be done." The man nods his balding head. "You can rest at my home until I have a space for you."

"A hot meal would be appreciated, for me and my companion."

The elder's eyes fall to Luminita, curled up against me. "Does she also require—"

"No," I interrupt.

Dumitru nods again but looks relieved. I suppose supplying willing donors to *two* strigoi might prove difficult.

"Is there a healer among you?"

"Minodora. She's a Dacian herb worker. I can send for her."

"Do that. For now, a warm fire and hot food will do. Perhaps some women's garments and blankets?"

"Follow me. My wife, Ioana, can help with the rest."

I urge John's horse forward at an easy pace, following Dumitru as he walks through the village.

"I notice you are not riding Kali tonight," the man says.

"She needed to rest. I just rode in from Belgrade days ago."

"Well, this is a fine beast as well."

I don't mention the Voivode for several reasons. Chief amongst them is the fact that they do not know I have any connection to him. They simply know me as Lord Aaron. It keeps a measure of anonymity between us.

When we reach the small house, I have no choice but to wake her. I tenderly caress her sunken cheek. "Luminita."

Her eyes flutter open, but she still appears exhausted. I find myself wondering how often she's slept…how often *he* allows her to sleep. Or perhaps it's merely the memories of what he's done that rob her of slumber.

"We're here. It's a safe place. They know me as Lord Aaron here."

She blinks up at me with muted blue eyes, and I'm not sure if she understands in her groggy state.

"Can you sit up long enough for me to dismount?"

Luminita draws in a breath and grips the pommel to pull herself upright.

I instantly miss her weight against my chest, but dismount quickly. I reach up, gripping her small waist. She places her hands on my shoulders this time. They stay there once her feet are on the ground, and she stares at me, searching my eyes or perhaps sifting through my emotions.

"What do you sense?" I ask, suddenly curious. Hopefully, she can understand them better than I can.

Her brow furrows slightly. "Sadness…heartache…" Her eyes fall to my chest. "Longing." She's silent for a moment, and her body trembles. "Why do you not feel disgust?"

The question takes me by surprise, shocking the truth from my lips. "Never, Draga." I pull her close, folding my arms around her. Hers circle my neck, and she clings to me. It ignites something warm in my chest, though I can't name it.

After a few minutes, I lean back and smooth the hair from her face. "*You* are still my goddess of blood and chaos. You always will be. I will bring you back to life, my beloved."

Luminita stiffens against me, her chest heaves, her face crumples, and fear grips my heart. "Not like that," she says in a whisper full of misery. "I can't." She swallows hard, shaking in my arms, and gods…my heart breaks *for* her this time.

The things he has robbed from her, ripped away, corrupted…

I hug her tight again before the rage takes over and press a kiss to her forehead. "I am asking nothing from you but to accept my help," I whisper against her skin.

Her shoulders shake, and a sobbing sound rips from her. "I don't deserve your help."

Tears fill my eyes, and I cradle her head against my heaving chest while struggling to take a full breath. Vlad's words come back to me then from the night I left for Belgrade. *You give her hope.* And then I left…this is the result. "You have it regardless. Always."

While her tears continue, I scoop her up in my arms again to carry her inside. Ioana, Dumitru's wife, brings blankets out to us while I sit before the fire with Luminita tucked in my lap. Once we're wrapped up in warmth and Ioana retires to another room to make food, I watch the flames dance like devils locked in combat.

Vlad breaking her spirit has been reason enough to hate him, but this…tormenting her nearly to the point of death, instilling such fear that even the thought of passion terrifies her… For *this*, Vlad will suffer.

My gaze drifts down to her face, turned toward the fire. She's stopped crying, but now only stares out despondently. I vowed to bring her back to life, but I feel it in my bones. This has forever changed her, darkened her, and I feel an odd thing in my chest. It's unfamiliar to me…at least when it comes to my own abilities—doubt.

21. The Vow

Luminita

Once the woman brings out the bowls of stew, Aaron lifts me in his arms again. They are a comfort I cannot refuse, even though I should. My body, my soul, even my decimated heart cries out for his touch, but my mental armor *must* stay in place. The horrors from Vlad broke me to the point of seeking death…if my blood caused that darkness in Aaron, it would shatter my very existence. Even the thought of it twists my insides into endless knots.

Aaron tenderly sets me in a chair and moves to sit across from me. He's worried. It's replaced some of the sadness he feels. Even if I couldn't sense those emotions, they are evident in every line of his handsome face. He loves me. And I…cannot afford to love him, even if I want to. I would only destroy him. My love is poison.

My watery eyes fall to the bowl in front of me, and nausea churns my guts. I push the bowl away from me and grab a piece of bread to pick at.

"Luminita, you *need* to eat," he says in a gentle voice while sliding the bowl back in front of me.

I place a small bit of bread in my mouth, which feels dry. "I feel sick. The bread will help."

His silvery eyes rake over my thin face again, and guilt emerges.

"Stop," I whisper, eyes on the stew steaming in front of me.

"What?"

"Feeling guilty. You did nothing wrong." The words sound hollow even to me, but not because I do not mean them. Because I know, if he tasted my blood, he might do wrong as well.

"I should have just killed the bastard the first time I laid eyes on him," Aaron mutters before taking a bite of stew.

My shoulders slump. "That would only have gotten you killed."

"Perhaps. But it would have spared you."

My eyes lift to his. "Only from his torments. I do not wish to witness *your* death."

A long sigh escapes him. "Is that why you drove me away that night?"

The bold question makes my heart race. How can I answer? If I am truthful, it will only bring him closer to me, which will endanger him more, but I do not wish to lie either.

I take a sip of water, still weighing my options, but he doesn't wait for my answer.

"You don't hate me," he states with confidence.

"No." The reply escapes me without thought.

"And you do care."

My armor falters, and I am too tired to weave lies tonight. "Yes."

When he says nothing else, I glance in his direction. His thumb rubs over the sleeve of his shirt while he stares down at his stew. "Please...try to eat more than bread."

I do as he asks. I can at least give him that. A few bites of meat and vegetables are all I can stomach before the nausea returns.

"Luminita—" Aaron begins, but when the man named Dumitru returns, he falls silent.

"Minodora will be here shortly, my Lord."

Aaron nods with a strained smile. When I peer at him curiously, he clarifies. "The herb worker. She's a healer."

"You and your companion are welcome to stay here in my home. Ioana and I will sleep at her sister's, but we will return in the morning to see to breakfast and anything else you need. Ana will also arrive shortly to provide what you require."

Aaron nods curtly. "Thank you."

Dumitru peeks over at me then, and an odd mix of sadness, pity, and wariness pulsates over his skin, but he says nothing else. The man strolls into the backroom, leaving us alone again.

"Ana?" I ask, suddenly curious.

Aaron keeps his eyes on his food. "Blood," he supplies in a flat tone as if feeding were merely a chore. "I pay the Elder of this town handsomely for willing donations. It keeps things discreet and away from John and the court."

Draga & the Savage: Dracul

I raise a brow, surprised. Two hundred years ago, Aaron didn't care for blending in. He took what he wanted…with one exception, of course. He followed the Mongol horde to indulge his bloodlust.

"The world has become a small place, and there is power in numbers. You know this. During battles, I can indulge. The men find it inspiring that I am such a brutal demon. But when I am forced to linger in the court with John between wars, I cannot embrace that side. That is why I ride here every other night, where they do not know me, and I pay for their discretion."

"Why stay in the court at all then?"

Aaron's gaze finally lifts. "For thousands of years, nothing seemed important but blood. Everything was but a flicker in my long life…not worth my notice. *You* taught me the value of a tiny moment. *You* taught me that three days can forever alter my course if I allow it. John is rather interesting for a human, and I find I enjoy his company most days. I suppose I wished to feel connected to something once again."

Guilt weighs heavily on my shoulders, and I cannot keep eye contact.

"You told me something once. *Follow me, Sălbatic, and I'll whisper my secrets while we tear a bloody path through the world.* Is that still your wish?"

Panic tears at my chest, and even drawing in a breath burns like the hottest fire. My mind screams to throw up those mental walls, to retreat and let fear take over my voice, to drive him away, but…I can't.

"Yes," I whisper in a voice so faint I'm not sure he even heard me.

Relief floods his signature, and I know then that he did.

I pull myself a little straighter and force my eyes to meet his. "I cannot give you everything you want. Perhaps not even most of what you want. But maybe together we can find a way to rise above the brutal laws of humans, to make ourselves invulnerable to them, to never suffer…" My voice breaks, and Aaron slips his hand over mine with a touch full of compassion.

"I will never allow it again. *Never.*"

I know he means it…at least, for now.

"You must make me one vow."

"Anything, Luminita."

My gaze locks on his, impressing the seriousness of my demand. "You can *never* taste my blood. Not a drop."

His brow furrows, but he nods. "I swear it. But…why?" A burning curiosity sparks in him, and my heart plummets. I should not have said anything.

"The reason does not matter. I simply need you to keep your word."

I can see the conflict in him.

"The night I left for Belgrade, Vlad confronted me. He asked me if I'd tasted you."

I swallow hard past the fear constricting my throat. "If you cannot simply swear it without explanation, I will not stay."

Aaron's hand slips away from mine, and the cold returns. "I have already sworn. I will not taste your blood, Luminita."

"My Lady," Dumitru's voice rouses me from the guilt weighing me down once again. "Minodora is here. She thought it best to see you in private. I can lead you to the bedroom."

Aaron moves to stand, but I grab his hand and rise to my feet.

"I can walk."

He's disappointed by this, and I am so tired of hurting him. I falter on my first step purposefully, and he's there in an instant to steady me. The feel of his arms wrapped around me brings me such peace, and I fight back my guilt. Was the ruse for his comfort or mine?

"Maybe I am still too weak," I whisper.

Aaron sweeps me up into his arms once more, and I relax against him, soaking in these moments like a glutton. It's unfair, but I am too tired to fight my own desires. He carries me into the bedroom where an old woman stands. The deep wrinkles lining her kind face draw together in a sympathetic frown.

"Place her on the bed, please. Then we must be alone."

Aaron doesn't move, and his fear becomes almost palpable.

"It's okay, Aaron." I point to the bundles of herbs laid out on the small table. "She can help me."

Reluctantly, he sits me on the bed. His hands cradle my face then, and he presses his forehead to mine. "I will wait just outside the door." Before he leaves, he softly kisses my cheek, and one of his tears lands there as well.

Once the door closes behind him, Minodora moves, selecting a bundle of sage from the table.

"You should disrobe," she says softly, and I comply. Saging has not worked to lessen the imprints Vlad left behind, but perhaps Minodora possesses more spirit than I.

When the woman turns back to me, she inhales sharply with a flood of horror. I am aware of why. Not being able to feed affects me in many ways…one of which is an inability to heal properly. Bruises and scars from Vlad's many abuses mar my pale skin stretched over my bones. I am just glad Aaron is not present to witness Vlad's masterpiece.

With time and regular feeding, these marks will disappear without a single trace. *They* are not what haunts me. It's the seething hatred steeped in sexual conquest clinging to my skin like leeches I need to be rid of.

22. Sacrifice

Aaron

I listen with my ear to the door and my heart pounding in my throat. When the herb worker gasps loud enough for me to hear her and says, "Dear gods, you poor child," I force myself to step away. My hands clench at my sides so tight it's painful.

"Lord Aaron, Ana has arrived."

I peer over at Dumitru with a thought and dig into my pocket. The man frowns when I pull out more gold coins.

"Sir. You've already paid more than enough."

"I require Ana for more than blood."

The man's frown deepens, creasing his wrinkled face. "What do you mean?"

I swallow hard and glance back at the closed door. Smoke trickles out from the cracks, and I hear chanting beyond. "I can't explain, but Ana may not survive. Is this sufficient?"

Dumitru stares at the ten florins in my palm for a long moment.

"My companion…she may not live without this sacrifice. I have more at my home if this is not enough for your discretion." Under any other circumstances, I wouldn't even ask. I would just take what we need, but Luminita is too weak. Staying here would be best for her. So, I resort to bribery.

The man glances at the door before meeting my eyes. "You have taken care of our village for quite some time, Lord Aaron. Your coin allows us to live in peace. For the greater good…" He releases a sigh. "I accept your terms. Ten is sufficient."

"Your dedication is noted and appreciated." I place the florins in his hand, and he stares at them for a moment. I understand his confliction, but this is merely an attempt to keep things peaceful. If I had to, I would slaughter the entire village to help her and feel no remorse. I'd prefer not to, of course. Things will be easier if the man simply agrees, but no one should mistake that for a conscience. I certainly do not.

"Ana awaits you near the fire," Dumitru says in an emotionless voice. "I will wait an hour outside in case I am required to…dispose of anything."

I nod brusquely before striding out to the front room. Ana waits by the fireplace, staring into its flickering depths. She is one of my frequent donors, a middle-aged widow with no children or family. That is why the elder selected her. Tonight, she has her muddy brown hair pulled up into a bun, revealing a collection of delicate scars along her neck.

Ana turns at the sound of my boots, and a nervous smile tugs at her thin lips before her gaze drops to the floor. "I am happy to be of service." The words lack any real warmth. Not that I blame her. This is a transaction. Nothing more.

"Sit." The command emerges a bit more clipped than intended. I dislike feeding this way. I miss the hunt. This is too much like my brother's idea of peace, hiding our nature. Unfortunately, my current life requires sacrifices.

The woman quickly moves to the table and sits stiffly in the chair.

"I would like to finish my stew while it's still warm." Not a complete lie, but I need to wait a little longer for the herb worker to finish her ritual.

"Of course, sir," she says quietly.

I slip into the opposite chair, keeping my eyes on my food. Spending time among humans is not something I am particularly fond of…with one rare exception—John.

"Elder Dumitru said you brought a guest?"

My eyes lift, and I peer up at her from beneath my heavy brow. "We don't need to talk."

"Yes, of course." The woman nervously plays with the hem of her sleeve while her eyes dart toward the door.

Perhaps a social interaction is required to keep her from bolting. A heavy sigh rushes past my lips, and I let the spoon clatter in the bowl. "I am being rude. My apologies."

When Ana turns back to stare at me in surprise, her full cheeks flush crimson. "Of course not, sir."

"Yes. I came with a companion. We will be staying a few days while Minodora tends to her."

"Your companion is unwell?" The woman suddenly appears concerned as if she knows Luminita. It's odd, this…sense of compassion for strangers that humans harbor. But in this case, it proves useful.

"Yes. I'm afraid she is. Very much so." I allow my worry and sadness to leak into my voice.

"I am so sorry, Lord Aaron. I shall pray for her."

Yes. Pray to the Christian god. The one who forsakes her. The one who sees no wrong with Vlad's vile actions. My jaw clenches, and I fight down the urge to yell at the woman. Luminita does not need her prayers. She needs something else entirely. I shovel a spoonful of stew into my mouth.

"Your companion…is she meant to be your wife?"

Internally, I groan at the question. I have only ever seen the human concept of marriage used for politics. Women are traded like cattle. Some like to romanticize it, dress it up as love. But Luminita is proof enough of what marriage truly is in this dismal place.

"No," I state with as little anger as possible. What Luminita and I share is a collision of souls. It always has been. I would not dare mar that with a claim of human ownership.

"Then she is family?" The woman asks.

Of course, that would be the only other socially acceptable reason for me to travel with a woman. Humans have such narrow thinking.

"Of sorts, I suppose," is my stiff reply.

Ana seems to sense my discomfort and falls silent, fingers working along her hem again.

The door in the back creaks open. I'm immediately on my feet. Minodora meets me halfway, and I peek around her at the half-closed door.

"I have done what I can for tonight," the herb woman says with a sad expression. "She needs rest. I will return in the morning."

"Thank you." It's not often I mean those words, but I do in this moment.

The woman bows her head, her stark white curls falling over her shoulders, and then shuffles off toward the door.

"Ana," I call, hoping she hasn't run off while I was distracted.

Thankfully, she hurries into the room. "Yes, sir."

"In the bedroom," I gesture forward, but the woman doesn't move. I rub a hand over my jaw, trying to contain my irritation. "I am *not* interested in violating you, if that is your concern."

Jenny Allen

Ana takes a few hesitant steps toward the door, but I've lost my patience. She most likely won't leave the room alive anyway. I grab her arm and pull her along. She screams and tries to fight, of course. They always do. But it's a useless endeavor. I've trained for battle my entire life. All seven thousand years.

When I enter the room, Luminita frowns up at me in confusion. The simple shift she wears hangs from her frail body, and it only steels my resolve.

I toss Ana forward, and Luminita's gaze follows. The weeping thing lands on her knees, and my battered goddess peers back up at me with a questioning look.

"I will take what I need, and then you will take what *you* need."

I snatch Ana, pulling her up to her feet, and pin her back to my chest.

Luminita says nothing. She merely stares at me.

Suddenly, the vivid memory takes over my thoughts. I stood in a circle with a maiden clutched to my chest. I watched Luminita as she chanted, firelight glimmering off her sheer crimson dress. A heated passion thrummed between us the night of Dragobete while I drank from my offering. The memory alone quickens my breath.

Ana continues to scream, but I barely hear it over the blood pounding in my ears. A flicker of light gleams in the eyes of my goddess as she stares at me. I wonder if she is recalling the same memory. Does it stir as much in her as it does in me?

I tug Ana's head to the side, keeping my gaze fixed on Luminita, and allow my fangs to unfold from the roof of my mouth. The delicate points pierce the flesh. Ana stills, her body stiffening.

I drink in several gulps, enough to sustain me, but I don't indulge. The sacrifice needs to be a strong one. I pull my mouth away from her neck and force the woman to her knees before my goddess, the only one worth worshipping.

"Take all you need."

Luminita stares up at me, her thin chest rising and falling rapidly. Perhaps the same memories continue to play in her mind. I can at least hope.

"Please, my lady," Ana pleads through sobbing tears, drawing my goddess's attention.

Luminita's frail hands caress the woman's tear-streaked face. "Shh, my child. You do not need to be afraid anymore," she says in gentle, soothing tones.

The sobbing cries slow…then they stop.

A soft sigh passes Luminita's lips, and her eyes drift closed. I watch in rapt fascination as her skin becomes less pale, her cheeks slightly less sunken, the circles around her eyes less pronounced. Luminita still looks ill and emaciated, but less so.

Ana's lifeless body collapses on the floor, and Luminita's eyes open, instantly meeting mine. They are a crisper blue. True hope fills my chest for the first time since I found her in the woods.

"You require more."

"Not tonight," she says in a breathy tone that sounds less raspy than earlier. "I am tired."

I avert my eyes to the floor and nod. "I'll remove this and allow you to sleep."

I bend to scoop up the woman's corpse, but Luminita's hand touches my arm, and I find her staring at me with tears in her eyes.

"May I ask you for something?"

"Yes," I abandon my task and kneel before my goddess instead.

Her tongue darts out, nervously wetting her lips. "Will you stay with me? Just…hold me while I sleep? Nothing else."

The request shocks me into silence.

The delicate column of her neck shifts with a hard swallow. "I know I have no right to ask so much, but—"

Before she can finish, my palms cradle her thin face. Every fiber of me wants to kiss her, but that is not what she asked of me. I press my forehead to hers again. "I will do anything my goddess of blood and chaos requires."

23.   Safe

Luminita

When Aaron leaves the room with the woman's body, Vlad's imprints seep back into my marrow. There are so many… The saging ritual didn't help much. The bite of his belt, the merciless slice of his knife, the sadistic desire of his wretched cock…they all squirm and writhe over my skin like poisonous maggots, constantly reminding me of his wicked deeds. Without a distraction…without something else to focus on…Vlad consumes me.

I should not have asked Aaron to lie with me. I *know* how he feels, how much he desires me…even *now*, like this, when he should be repulsed by my frailty and weakness. However, I also know that without him, sleep will never find me. I'll be alone with my demons, and I don't have the strength for that. Selfish *and* weak.

I tell myself it's temporary. I'm already feeling stronger, but…will I *ever* be strong enough to send Aaron away, to sever our ties, to save him from me? *That* I doubt very much.

It's not long, thankfully, until the door swings open. Aaron steps inside and pauses. "Do you…want anything before bed? Wine perhaps?" Something peculiar trickles into his signature. I only recall sensing the emotion once in Deva—nervousness. I notice his fingers rub against the cuff of his shirt like they had earlier.

"Dumitru left a bottle," Aaron says when I remain silent.

"That would be nice." I pull on a small smile, and he relaxes. I don't need the drink, but he obviously does. Aaron has done so much already, and perhaps the wine will help me sleep more soundly. I can at least hope.

The corners of his mouth lift, subtly revealing the dimples that bracket his mouth. He bows his head and disappears for a moment.

Aaron returns with a bottle and two wooden cups, still wearing the same slight smile. A fragile sort of hope clings to him, and tonight, I don't wish to break it. He pours a generous amount into both cups before handing me one.

I stare into its dark depths with memories of Dragobete. We'd collided with such divine passion, it shook the world…mine and his, at least. But then I put the chalice to his lips, made him drink the poisoned wine, all to keep from losing myself.

Then I allowed Vlad to slowly destroy me over the years, and I lost myself regardless.

"I didn't poison it. No Datura seeds. I swear."

My eyes snap up, expecting anger from an old wound, but Aaron wears a sly grin, his silvery eyes sparkling in the candlelight.

"I did not expect you to *ever* find it humorous."

His smile slips, becoming less genuine. "I don't. I believe we *both* lost something that night. But I find the ironic parallels between then and now…amusing. I suppose."

I lock my eyes with his and drink deep from my cup. "I do trust you," I say sincerely.

It does not seem to relieve him the way I hoped. "To a point, perhaps," he corrects in a sad tone.

"As much as I can," I state firmly. "Which is more than I can say for *anyone else.*"

Aaron nods and drains his cup in one long gulp.

I place mine on the ground, too tired to remain sitting. After climbing into the bed, I lie down facing the wall. Candlelight flickers across its surface, and Aaron's silhouette moves.

The mattress dips, and fear instinctively floods my system. Panic squeezes my chest and pulls every muscle taut. I struggle to shove it all down. *This is not Vlad behind me*, I repeat to myself in an endless chant.

Both of Aaron's arms slip gently around me. Then he slowly pulls me toward him, hugging my back to his chest. Aaron surrounds me with warmth, and the chanting in my head recedes.

His breath rushes across my neck with each exhale, sending goosebumps over my flesh. One by one, my muscles relax. For the first time in years, they aren't tensed in a perpetual state of fearful anticipation.

Draga & the Savage: Dracul

Drowsiness drags me closer to sleep. Aaron's nose nestles into my hair, and he whispers soothing words. I'm too tired to make sense of them, but the low rumble of his voice lulls me to sleep.

When I wake, Aaron's warm arms are still wrapped tight around me. His chest presses against my back with each deep inhale, and my hair rustles with every slow exhale. The steady rhythm is comforting. I could stay cocooned like this in his arms for days, but my body is not so inclined.

The wine moves quickly through my system. With a soft groan, I force myself to move, twisting to face Aaron. The sight of him makes me pause.

The unguarded moment allows me to study him in a way I have never been able to. Sleep softens his typically rigid features, and a slight smile lifts one side of his mouth. It must be a pleasant dream. I have not had one of those in quite some time.

His stubble is thicker now, more of a close-clipped beard than when we first met. Aaron's dark lashes seem longer, too, but perhaps I didn't notice them before now. The faint streaks of grey in his dark hair are only slightly more pronounced than they were two hundred years ago. His chest and shoulders seem broader. Years of waging war have sculpted him into an even more impressive specimen.

My palm hovers over his cheek, not quite touching the skin, but skimming along his energy. I watch my fingers dance along the glow of contentment surrounding him. I'm tempted to draw on it…steal it for myself, but my power does not work that way. If I take his contentment, it only becomes energy to me. I don't take on the emotion. Besides, I would not steal this from him. It's rare and fleeting, and…he has suffered for it—*will* suffer even more for it if I don't let him go.

"Some people consider it impolite to stare."

His voice startles me, and my gaze snaps back to his face. Aaron's eyes study me while an amused grin curls his lips.

Despite—or perhaps because of—everything I've endured, the thought of falling into him is far too tempting.

Aaron's hand glides over my hip in a soft caress. The same energy that has drawn us together since we met tugs at me now, urging me toward him, begging me to lose myself in this moment.

I push away with an exaggerated groan as if he is being tedious. Once I escape his arms, I crawl down the bed.

"Where are you going?" Fear traces his voice…fear I instilled in him.

After getting to my feet, I peer over my shoulder. "I need to pee. I think I can handle that on my own."

Despite my irritable tone, his grin widens. The man is infuriatingly charming at times.

When I pad back through the door moments later, I find Aaron still lying in the bed. His contemplative stare is locked on the ceiling, and his fingers rub at the same spot on his right cuff. I've seen him do that many times since I first visited Beszterce, but I don't recall the habitual motion from our time in Deva.

"What has you so deep in thought?" I ask, honestly curious.

Aaron's gaze darts to me with an edge of nervousness. "Nothing," he replies quickly, before sitting up. "It's still early." Aaron rubs his face as if physically trying to wipe away his thoughts. "You should rest more." When I don't speak or move, his studious gaze scans over me. "You still look tired."

"I am," I admit while pacing closer. I sit on the bed beside him, wrapping my arms around myself.

We sit in silence for a while. It isn't precisely uncomfortable, but I feel the weight of things unsaid.

Finally, Aaron breaks the quiet. "You cannot go back to him."

I swallow hard, recognizing the truth of his words, but I can't seem to speak.

Aaron turns toward me and lifts my chin until my eyes meet his. "I won't let you. I would rather tie you to this bed and have you hate me forever than allow that monster to touch you one more time." Conviction forges each word that passes his lips into an iron-clad promise.

The independent part of me screams against the dominating threat, but even my fear is tired tonight. I can't make myself push him away…can't summon the energy to lash out…can't bring myself to cause him pain.

My hands run up his bearded cheeks, the stiff hair tickling my palms. "I know," I whisper. In a truly selfish moment, I capture his lips in a tender, lingering kiss before leaning my forehead against his. Tears fill my eyes as I wish this moment wasn't fleeting…that I could make it last without putting us both in danger. "Thank you, Sălbatic, for saving my life."

Aaron's arm wraps around me, pulling me close, and I tuck my head under his chin. The steady beat of his heart greets me, and I close my eyes to savor it.

When Aaron's hand caresses down my back, however, his heart races wildly. He stills. I know why. The thin shift can't pad the welts and cuts on my back. There are *many*…and the energy I stole from the woman did little to heal them.

"I swear to you, Luminita Dragomir, I *will* make him pay. Whatever it takes."

I say nothing, but curl closer to him. It's the only place I feel safe.

24.   The Choice

Aaron

Containing my rage is nearly impossible. I want to spare Luminita from feeling it, but the map of sadistic pain on her back stirs dark urges to rend Vlad Dracul into unrecognizable pieces. It was one thing to hear the healer's gasp and exclamations of horror. It is quite another to feel the marks beneath my fingertips. There are *so many*, and each one stabs at my heart like a poisoned dagger.

She's asleep again, curled up in my lap with her gaunt face pressed to my chest. My fingers drift through her raven-black curls in soothing strokes, but my mind is busy.

In a few days, I'll have to return to Beszterce. John is expecting me *and* his horse. I have no doubt he'll want me to ride with him, raising an army for the coming battle in Belgrade. Normally, I'd be eager for the bloody fray, but…

My gaze falls to Luminita's face. Even after draining Ana, she's still so thin, so weak. Leaving her for a day or two will be hard enough. I won't abandon her for a war I don't truly care about. I'd rather march on Sibiu and rip Vlad's spine from his body.

John won't like my decision, of course. Turning my back on the Kingdom of Hungary for the sake of a married woman. In human eyes, it will be blasphemy, perhaps even treason, but I hope he'll still help me.

There is only one escape for the Lady Katharina Dracul. If Vlad believes she is dead, Luminita Dragomir can finally be free.

My mind works over every angle while she sleeps, my fingers idly stroking her hair. What must be hours pass, and I hear a door open. Shuffling footsteps draw nearer to the bedroom. I can already tell they belong to Minodora.

When she knocks, I tell her to enter, and the door creaks open. The old woman's face pulls into a sympathetic smile when she spots us on the bed.

"Good. She sleeps. I wasn't certain she'd be able to after..." The words trail off, but she doesn't need to say them. We both know what happened...what Luminita has endured...what *Vlad* has done to her.

"I gave her some wine." My eyes drift back down to Luminita, sleeping soundly. She almost looks peaceful.

"I'm sure *that* is what helped."

When I peer back up, Minodora flashes a knowing smile before laying out her selection of herbs.

"What are they for?" I ask, suddenly curious.

"Sage is the most important. The smoke cleanses the spirit and the space, removing negative energies. Sometimes, a cleansing alone helps heal."

"But not in this case?" I ask, finishing her rather obvious thought.

A somber expression pulls at the deep lines in her face. "What happened to her...it has occurred over years, has it not?"

"It has. At least four."

The woman nods, her fingers trailing over a bundle of dried herbs I don't recognize. There aren't many that I do, to be honest.

"*Can* she heal from it?" I find myself asking.

"Physically, yes...over time. Emotionally... Well, that is up to her. She is the only one who can make the choice to either hide from the world or fearlessly live within it, despite what was done to her. Many pick the former."

I nod softly and peer back down at my wounded goddess. She sleeps so deeply. I hate to wake her. My fingertips coast along her cheek, her jaw, her bottom lip.

"Draga," I say softly, almost hoping she doesn't hear me.

Her eyes flutter open, and she struggles to focus.

"Luminita. Minodora is here."

A soft sound escapes her. It's something between a moan and a breathy groan, which immediately summons a deep desire in me. I can't help it, even though I know it's unwanted in this moment.

Luminita's eyes open fully then, most likely sensing the sudden shift in my emotions, and she frowns up at me. Her sea-blue eyes silently scold me, but...she subtly bites at her bottom lip, fighting a smile. *That* does not help matters.

"I should get you some water before you start." Once I have Luminita sitting upright, I slip off the bed and leave the room, trying to will my blood to stop rushing to the most inconvenient place possible.

Honestly, after holding her against me through the night, it's rather surprising it wasn't an issue sooner. It doesn't matter how thin or wounded she appears. Luminita is and will always be *my* goddess. Her very essence affects me in a way no other ever has.

However, that is *not* what Luminita wants or needs from me now. After what she endured…she may never want that from me. I've gone thousands of years without sex, I try to remind myself.

Of course, none of those years truly tested me. For two hundred years, I have been crawling out of my skin with need after being in her presence for three days. I have longed for only her ever since we first met.

A thousand years at Luminita's side without being able to touch her, kiss her, enjoy her to the fullest? Now *that* I may not survive. The thought at least sobers me enough to regain control of my body.

After pouring water into a cup, I pad back to the bedroom. Minodora is already fanning the sage smoke into the air. Thankfully, Luminita has not discarded her shift. I'm relieved. Primarily because I don't think I could handle seeing the evidence of Vlad's abuse.

Luminita's gaze lifts to me with a soft smile, and I hand her the cup. "Thank you, Aaron." Gratitude floods her eyes as she takes a deep drink before passing it back to me. I know her thanks are not simply for the water.

Since I found her in the woods, she has been so…open, honest, vulnerable. I want so badly to believe that perhaps I've slipped past the mental armor she wears. But the healer's words echo in my head, and I fear this is a fleeting moment between us. I cannot truly blame her for wanting control after Vlad ripped it away so violently. But…I wish I could make her see that we could be different. Equals.

Without another thought, my fingers slide into her hair, and I bend to press a lingering kiss to her forehead. Her palm strokes my cheek, and the simple touch soothes my racing heart. Maybe there is hope. Maybe this is our way through.

With a conflicted heart, I wander back out to the front room, leaving them to their ritual.

Over an hour passes while I pace the small area. Dumitru and Ioana arrive and begin making food. We don't speak, and I don't stop pacing until Minodora finally emerges. The herb worker informs me she will return tonight and leaves.

When I make my way back to the bedroom, I find Luminita sitting on the mattress with her back to me. "Dumitru and Ioana will have food ready soon."

Her head dips, but she doesn't look back at me or turn around.

"Does it help? The herbs?"

"Some," she says quietly.

"How does it help?" I ask curiously.

Luminita is quiet. But when I open my mouth to try again, she finally speaks.

"Do you recall how I found you after Timisoara?"

"You followed the trail of my hunger," I reply.

"Strong emotions leave an imprint. One I can feel for quite some time. Years…even centuries."

The implications of her words hit like a broadsword to my gut.

"The sage helps mute them…helps them fade faster."

"Is there anything else that can help?" After seven thousand years of life, feeling useless is not a familiar emotion. Knowing Luminita is not only suffering but surrounded by Vlad's hateful emotions, and that I may be powerless to help her, is a new sort of torment for me.

Her face turns, but not fully. "No."

There is an odd, almost hesitant tremor in her voice, but I don't press the issue. "Is there anything I can get you?"

"No, Aaron. I just need to be alone for a few moments." Even her voice sounds distant, and that gnawing dread I've been ignoring starts to grow. I fear she is slowly making the choice to hide.

"I'll come get you when the food is ready."

Her head dips again, but she says nothing.

When we sit at the table, she manages to eat a decent amount, but she's quiet. I try a few times to talk about things, but beyond a few simple answers, she merely nods. Afterwards, she sits by the fire, watching it dance for hours.

I make another deal with Dumitru for a sacrifice I can share with Luminita. The man is uncomfortable with the idea, but the temptation of more coin persuades his conscience. I give him my word that when I return from Beszterce, I will pay my debts.

Crina arrives later that evening. She is another childless woman of the village who has donated to me on previous occasions. Minodora has already completed her second session with Luminita, so pleasantries are not required tonight.

As soon as the plump woman enters, I grip her arm tight and slam the door closed. The silent shock doesn't last long after I begin dragging her toward the bedroom. This one manages a swift kick to my knee, however. With an angry growl, I toss the woman over my shoulder and stalk back to the bedroom with a slight limp.

Humans are so protective of their short lives even when they're steeped in misery. But only one person's life…one person's misery matters to me, and it is not Crina's.

I dump her rather unceremoniously on the floor, and the thing weeps. Luminita studies me as I pull the woman upright and crouch down.

"For us to share," I state simply.

The hungry glint in her eye is muted compared to last night, which only stirs my sadness and frustration. Still, I hold her gaze as my fangs and teeth sink into the screaming woman's neck. When I've taken what I need, Luminita scoots closer and grips the woman's tear-streaked face. I can feel Crina's body cool beneath my hands as I hold her in place.

Luminita's head tilts back and her eyes close as if savoring a delicious meal, and I watch, transfixed. After a moment, her eyes open and find mine. They are a touch brighter than before, and her cheeks are less gaunt with a slightly rosy hue.

"After you dispose of her, will you come to bed?"

I'm almost surprised by the question after she's been so distant today. "Of course."

When I return, she is already lying down, facing the wall. I slip into the bed and feel her body tense when my hands first reach for her. Then she relaxes against me with a heartbreakingly soft sigh. My arms wrap around her, holding her tight, and we both drift to sleep.

25. Madness

Luminita

Darkness fills the room like a suffocating presence. Hatred and malice writhe over my skin like snakes, leaving stinging bites in their wake. I am hunched over my knees, arms outstretched before me, wrists tied to the headboard. It is an all too familiar position. I don't dare move or fight. Doing so only makes things worse.

Vlad's hands slide down my back with sadistic pleasure, seeking an unblemished bit of skin to mar. My entire body tenses at his touch, bracing for what is to come. Distantly, I realize this is a nightmare, but it is still real. It still happened…*many* times.

I hear his belt snap tight and instinctively tremble in response. I hate that I give him that reaction, the one he desires so much. His rough hand rubs over the curve of my hip with a stomach-churning groan, and the sickness of his lust further twists my guts.

When he rocks his hips against me and I feel him hard and ready, disgust and hatred burn through my veins. Vlad knows, of course, and retaliates with a sharp snap of his belt across my shoulders. The welt immediately burns and pulls a whimper from my lips.

His hand grips my throat, pulling my head back, and he leans in close to whisper while his sickeningly hard length presses against me. "Am I not savage enough for you?"

I hate hearing that word from his vile lips. I know why he does it. The thought of my savage, my Sălbatic, gives me hope, and Vlad has made it his mission to corrupt that beyond repair. Perhaps he already has.

Hot breath washes over my neck, and terror immediately clenches my stomach. Two sharp points rake over the delicate scar tissue he's left behind. He won't let me heal. He wants to see the results of his handiwork.

One hand slips between us, positioning himself, and even though I know better, I try to squirm away from him. His fingers tighten on my throat until I can barely drag in a breath.

"That's it, my love. Fight. You crave the pain."

Nails dig into my neck, and I feel the trickle of blood down my skin. I stop fighting and simply try to drag a wisp of air into my lungs.

As he buries himself inside me for the hundredth time, he leans heavily against my back, his tongue snaking out to lick at the blood on my neck. Then he purrs against my ear with dark delight.

"Your blood is madness, my love. One taste and you brought me to life." The quality of his voice changes as he speaks, and my blood turns to ice. Dread blossoms in my chest as I peer over my shoulder. It is no longer Vlad behind me with a wrathful grin of vengeance.

The sight of Aaron's grey eyes lit with violent need sends me spiraling out of the dream, and I wake sobbing and fighting for air. Candlelight flickers through the empty room as I scramble into the corner, drawing my knees up to my chest. Every labored breath is a struggle, and the imprints from Vlad seem more vibrant on my skin, pulsing and burning, as if worked into a frenzy. A cold sweat breaks over me. I squeeze my eyes shut, trying to picture anything else, *anything* besides Aaron's horrifying gaze lit with Vlad's malice.

For the first time in days, I'm grateful to be alone.

My trembling hands rub the tears from my face. I can still feel the bite of the rope on my wrists. My blood is madness…even to me.

With slow, measured breaths, I work diligently to shove every riotous emotion into that deep, dark pit in my mind. The stronger ones resist my efforts, but eventually, detached calm settles over me, and the vise around my chest loosens.

The door quietly opens, and my gaze snaps up, fear immediately escaping the mental pit. Aaron peeks inside. His confusion reaches me first as he peers at the seemingly empty bed. Then he spots me in the corner. When his eyes meet mine, the gut-wrenching fear seizes my insides, and I bury my face in my hands.

"Luminita? What's wrong?" His voice is gentle, but the nightmare still tears at my mind, corrupting his image. I hear him step closer, and panic tightens my chest.

"Stop. I need to be alone." The words are a desperate plea that only makes him move faster toward me.

I feel him reach for me, and I shrink further into the corner. "Do not touch me!" I shriek.

He hesitates, the warmth of his hand still hovering over my shoulder.

"Leave!" My fear takes over, snapping at him like a snarling wolf.

Pain and heartache flood my senses in an overwhelming torrent, and it's too much.

"Get out! I want to be alone!"

His hand recoils, and relief washes over me. I pant for air as the panic eases enough for me to breathe. He says nothing, but I hear his footsteps retreating from the room, taking his anguish with him. I cannot bear it. I have enough of my own.

Once the door creaks closed, I lay my head back against the wall and gaze at the thatched ceiling. Vlad's words repeat in my mind on an endless loop. *Your blood is madness, my love.* I feel the truth of it in my very marrow.

Even now, with Vlad miles away, he steals the only comfort I had left, my only solace, the only thing that helped quell the imprints more than the sage ritual—Aaron's loving embrace.

I stay in the room the entire day. Minodora comes and goes. The sage rituals do little to mute the horror in my thoughts today. Aaron checks on me several times, bringing food and water, but I ignore his presence. Each time I face the wall, refusing to even look at him. I can't, not while the terrifying image from my nightmare is still so fresh in my mind. I know it hurts him, which only makes my inner torment worse.

That night, he brings another sacrifice. I still face the wall, despite his pleas. I can't watch tonight. The thought of his fangs buried in my neck sends a cold chill through my body. Once he's had his fill, he leaves the weeping man on the floor, exits the room, and closes the door.

As soon as we're alone, I slide off the bed and sink my hands into the man's hair. His shock only registers for a moment. I picture Vlad in my mind and viciously tear away every shred of vitality. In seconds, the man collapses to the ground, and strength infuses my body. The energy glows within me, forcing all my emotions back into the pit until I feel numb once more.

The door creaks open again, and Aaron steps inside. I don't turn away this time, but I stare fixedly at the floor.

"I have to leave for Besztercze tomorrow," he says in a strained voice. I can hear his tears, but I say nothing.

"I'll only be gone a few days. Three at most."

I dip my head to show my understanding. The news has conflicting emotions clawing at the edge of the pit.

"I don't want to leave," he says softly.

"Do what you must." My voice sounds hollow even to me.

"Do you *want* me to leave?" A fragile hope infuses his question, and despite the nightmare still haunting me, I cannot bring myself to utterly destroy it.

"No."

"Do you want me to hold you tonight?" The vulnerability in him makes my pulse race. I want so desperately to say yes, but the memory of his face wearing Vlad's violent expression refuses to allow me.

Tears constrict my throat until air barely passes. I draw my knees up to my chest and shake my head, unable to form the words.

Pain and anguish spill into the room, and a tear streaks down my cheek. I hear him move closer, and I tense, but he doesn't reach for me. I hear the body dragging across the floor, and then the door closes, leaving me alone with Vlad's torments.

26. Larissa

Aaron

My makeshift bed of blankets in front of the fire reminds me of our room in Deva. I refused to sleep on the floor that night. In fact, I threatened to leave if she didn't share the bed…as if I could have upheld the threat. My gaze drifts to the back of the house, and the emotional dagger in my chest twists, driving a little deeper.

Gods, she couldn't even look at me tonight. She said she doesn't want me to leave, but…she didn't want me to stay either. I don't know what changed. She's barely spoken all day, ever since I found her huddled in the corner. Maybe the emotional impressions Vlad left on her skin were worse today. The thought that he is still able to torment her to such a degree without being present sickens my stomach.

I close my eyes against the burning tears. *Some choose to hide from the world*, Minodora had said. Is that what Luminita is doing? Hiding? Even from me? Is that the future my goddess has chosen? Perhaps she merely needs more time. That is one thing we both have in abundance…at least, in theory. I've waited two hundred years…I can wait longer.

The ghost of a laugh passes my lips. *I can wait*, as if it's a choice. Luminita Dragomir is the only creature to move me to tears, to make me long for her in torment, to make me seek permission, to steep me in a near ravenous desire, to make my heart *feel*, to add color to this dreary world of misery. *She* is what matters to me. Time will not change that. Nothing will.

I'll wait because there is no other option. I am hers, regardless of whether she wants me. If only she could understand the truth…how much of my life I'm willing to lay at her feet.

I curl toward the fire, watching the flames' hypnotic dance, praying it will lull me to sleep. Of course, it has the opposite effect. All I see is Luminita in that sheer crimson dress on the night of Dragobete. The ethereal way she moved, firelight glinting off the gold bands, the dress glowing around her naked silhouette like a sacred flame, chanting the Dionysian rite with such fervor…it made me a true believer in her divinity. She was magic wrapped in an irresistible form, a force of nature, a goddess among the weak, an impossibility.

Soft footsteps sound behind me, and my body tenses. For a moment, I don't dare breathe, terrified I've imagined it, that she isn't really there.

Bare feet pad around me, and my breathing quickens. When Luminita sinks to her knees, her red-rimmed eyes find mine with a silent plea. Even now, in her delicate state, her vulnerability, she is fierce and beautiful.

The lump of flesh in my chest, which belongs solely to her, thrashes against my ribs in violent demand. I lift my arm, inviting her closer, but say nothing. She stares at me, seconds stretching into minutes, and my fragile hope begins to crack.

Then she slowly crawls toward me, avoiding my stare, and nestles into my arms. I can finally draw in a full breath for what seems like the first time today. Her tear-streaked cheek presses to my chest, and I let my arm fall softly over her shoulder, holding her loosely.

Luminita's body trembles, and she burrows closer, firmly pressing her body against mine. I hug her tight to me, clinging to her with relieved tears in my eyes, but still say nothing. I'm frightened of shattering this moment. It may be all I ever have.

With that realization, I rest my cheek on her head and close my eyes. I memorize the warm weight of her against me, the way she trembles, the scent of sage in her hair, her steady breathing, even the tears she leaves on my skin.

Eventually, she lulls me to sleep with a feeling of contentment. I only hope she finds a fraction of the same comfort in me.

When I wake in the morning, my arms are empty. For a few moments, I wonder if I dreamed the entire thing. Then the scent of sage fills my nostrils. I can smell it on my clothes…on my skin. I didn't imagine it, but she isn't here now.

With a heavy sigh, I push off the floor and wander around the house, but find no sign of her. A bubble of panic begins to form in my chest, and I rush for the front door, praying she didn't just leave. For someone who doesn't believe in God, I seem to be praying an awful lot these days.

I find her standing by the road, staring at the rising sun, a blanket wrapped around her shoulders. It's the first time she's been outside since we arrived. My panic eases, and I stroll out to stand beside her.

"You're leaving for Beszterce today?" she says softly, eyes still on the sunrise.

"Yes," I reply with a regretful sigh. "I need to return John's horse and take care of a few things."

"What things?"

I draw in a deep breath and release it slowly. "There is only one way to truly free you. Vlad needs to believe you are dead."

She nods as if she expected my answer. I'm not really surprised. Luminita is an exceptionally bright woman.

"And then what will we do?"

We. My thoughts halt on that word. "We'll plot. Together. Figure out a way to destroy the man."

Again, she nods, but this time she turns to face me. Her luminous sea-blue eyes lift until they reach mine, and she studies me for a moment. "And you will keep your oath to me?"

My brow furrows. "Of course. I gave you my word, something I don't give many people. I will never take your blood without permission. Ever."

Her gaze lowers then, as if some mental war rages in her mind. "Minodora will be here shortly. Will you wait to leave until we are finished?"

A sudden boldness overtakes me, and I tenderly cradle her face, tilting it back up toward me. Once our gazes lock. I speak only the truth. "I will *always* wait for you, Luminita."

Her deep eyes water, and she leans into my chest. I wrap my arms around her, close my eyes, and memorize every detail of the moment.

Minodora arrives and performs her sage ritual while I pack and saddle John's warhorse. Dumitru and his wife made us food and brought me provisions for the ride. If I push the horse, I should make the trek by nightfall. I'll speak with John, make arrangements, stay the night, and ride back at first light, assuming everything goes to plan. I just have one stop to make in town before I head out.

Once everything is ready, I head back into the house. Minodora greets me just inside the door.

"Luminita said you're leaving today?"

"Only for a few days. It can't be helped."

The old woman nods, her smile crinkling her wrinkled face. "I will look after her for you. I will stay the night. That is the worst time for her."

"Thank you."

The woman flashes another smile and reaches up to pat my cheek. "You are a good man."

No one has ever accused me of that, and if she knew my plans, I doubt she'd still think so. But for the sake of peace, I merely smile and bow my head before heading to the back room.

Luminita stands in the room's center, pulling her shift back into place. One shoulder is exposed until she pulls the fabric, and I catch a glimpse of the scars. They immediately summon a deep and loathing hatred for the bastard who hurt her…repeatedly…with a blade, belt, and flame, judging by the scars.

Luminita spins, her eyes wild and her chest heaving with panicked breaths. My cheeks blaze, and my gaze darts to the floor while I try to contain the sudden rage consuming me, the rage she no doubt felt.

"I'm sorry. I should have given you more time." I hurry through the words, hoping this doesn't sever our tenuous bond.

Footsteps pad closer until she stops in front of me. Reluctantly, I move my gaze to her, frightened of what I'll see. Luminita rarely reacts the way I expect her to. Of course, that is one of the things that drew me to her in the first place.

Luminita straightens under my stare, reclaiming a glimmer of the strong, proud goddess I once knew. "You are ready?"

I dip my head, and her breaths quicken.

"And you won't be gone long?" I can't be certain, but her voice seems to tremble slightly.

"I'll return as fast as I can."

The delicate column of her throat shifts, and it sends my heart racing. My body simply reacts without thought. My hand slips over her cheek, cradling her nape, and I pull her toward me. To my amazement, her lips meet mine in a kiss so tender it's almost torturous. Every part of me wants to deepen the kiss, haul her into my arms, pin her against the wall, and finish what we started in Beszterce, but I don't. It isn't my lust she needs right now…it's my compassion.

I break the sensual kiss to press my forehead to hers. "You'll be safe here. Dumitru and Minodora will look after you. I'll return soon, and when I do, Draga, you will finally be free."

I close my eyes, inhale her scent of sage deep into my lungs, and turn away. I don't look back. I stride for the door…for John's horse before I lose my will and lock myself in that room with her. There is work to be done. I *have* to leave, but gods…it's the last thing I want to do.

Once I mount, I spur the horse toward the edge of town, to the little hovel on the hill. A petite woman comes out to greet me with a brilliant smile. Her raven black hair falls to her waist in cascading curls, and her deep blue eyes shine in the morning sun.

Larissa has been fascinated by me since my arrival years ago, but I never accepted her as a donor. Mostly, because she reminded me too much of my goddess. Lesser men might have taken advantage of that fact, lived out a fantasy, but the similarities twisted my stomach. She is a human, a poor imitation of divinity, a vessel without a soul. I could never believe she is my goddess.

"Lord Aaron. What brings you here today?" I can sense the hope in her voice, which only irritates me further.

"I have need of you," I state in a brusque tone as I dismount.

"You do?" Another bright smile curves her lips, and I lose my patience for small talk.

I stride up to her purposefully, and when my hands slip around her neck, her blue eyes widen.

"What do you need?" Excitement abandons her, leaving only fear behind.

"Your corpse," I reply simply. Before the words register, I snap her neck. The body starts to fall, but I catch it in my arms and carry it back to the horse. The hour is still early, and Larissa's hovel doesn't sit close to the others. I doubt anyone saw our little exchange.

After slinging the body across the horse, right behind my saddle, I secure it with a bit of rope, so it doesn't fall while I'm galloping for Beszterce. Once I mount, I survey the surrounding area, but spot no one watching. I turn the horse back toward the road and ride hard.

To be continued in
Draga & the Savage: Corvinus

About the Author

Jenny Allen (Deardorff), the author of The Lilith Adams Series, also published poems and short stories in University journals while spending time as a reporter and photographer for the Chattanooga State College newspaper. Ms. Allen studied forensic science, compiled extensive research in world myths, and applied them into a thrilling supernatural series. Her background as a published photographer and award-winning artist helps her visualize scenes when writing, contributing to her unique style of vivid imagery.

Born on a Royal Airbase in Lakenheath, England, she left the U.K. at age nine to travel the United States and Germany. In her sophomore year, she began writing poetry after the suicide of a close friend. She later graduated to short stories and narratives until, in 2002, she wrote her first novel, Lilith in London, which was never published but still exists as 432 handwritten pages. Over twelve years, it underwent a metamorphosis, eventually becoming her first published novel, Blood Lily.

Currently, Mrs. Allen (Deardorff) lives in York, Pennsylvania with her husband, Eric Deardorff, and their two sons, Kaidan and River. When not working as a full-time RN, she is writing and plotting the remaining novels in the main series, the novella series, and the spin-off series with Tim and Eileen, all in the same world.

9 798989 249268